# Candace Gold's
# Book Shorts

## Stories for a Quick Read
## 5 New Short Stories

A Cruise to Remember

After Claudia Rybeck's mother passes from cancer, she goes on a well-deserved cruise. She meets a handsome guy, Blake Henry, but loses his attention to a wealthy woman named Abigail Arnold. She doesn't have long to feel sorry for herself before she meets the Dean of Students, Charles Roberson. They date and soon become a couple.

Nearly a year later, Claudia reads an article in the newspaper about the accidental death of Abigail Arnold and her grieving husband, Blake Henry. She recalls Blake telling her that his first wife had died in an accident, as well. This stokes her curiosity and she contacts a childhood friend in law enforcement. But is she prepared for what she What discovers and its consequences?

Married to a Stranger

When Marisa Martin tells her husband, Paul she is pregnant, he is thrilled. Only after the baby is born, it isn't long before he resents the infant. He complains that Paul Jr. is annoying and high jacking his time away from Marisa. Their relationship soon suffers, and they grow apart. Paul files for divorce and shocks Marisa by suing for custody of the baby. With no source of income other than Paul, how will she fight to keep her son?

Now and Forever

When Jamie Connelly receives a call that her mother was hospitalized and critical, she purchases a ticket for the first flight out of Newark heading to Minnesota. At lunch when her husband, Michael sees a special news broadcast concerning the crash of the plane Jamie had taken, his entire world stops revolving. And when the official word came that there were no survivors, he is devastated. He is filled with hope, though, when he discovers that for reasons unknown, Jamie wasn't on that flight. However, that hope is quickly extinguished when he is notified by the police that Jamie had been killed in an auto accident.

Michael can't move on with his life. No woman could ever fill Jamie's place. Then a friend asks him if Jamie had a sister. He encountered a woman resembling Jamie recently. Jamie had no sister which brings Michael hope that somehow she is still alive. However, is this just false hope or could Jamie still be alive?

Turning Back the Hands of Time

When Rachel Taylor ran away from her hometown six years earlier to forget the guy who hurt her and the father who disowned her, she never expected the one phone call out of the blue that could make her return to the place that brought her such grief. A classmate, now a nurse, informs Rachel that her father is dying from cancer. Does she have the strength to visit him in the hospital— especially if he may turn her away? And face her other demons?

Walk On By

Marlene Greene finally decides to sell her house after her husband Ron dies and move into a new assisted-living complex. The day she goes to sign the lease, she runs into her first love, Rich Flynn, who abruptly dropped her for someone else. The devastation she'd buried deep in her psyche comes rushing back at her so severely that she wants to back out of her lease. Will she find the strength to remain there despite seeing the man who'd hurt her so or choose to run away?

# A CRUISE TO REMEMBER
by Candace Gold

It was both a curse and a blessing. I couldn't believe Mom was gone after having been the center of my life for such a long time. We'd always shared the good and bad times together, though some would say our relationship had been more parasitic with her keeping me from living my own life. Perhaps. The jury is still deliberating. What I am certain of, is that her death left a gaping hole in the fabric of my very existence. I'd never married, so there was no husband or children to help me fill it with love. And every passing day, which I managed to live through, it was a constant reminder. Even going to the supermarket was Mom's thing. She'd love running into neighbors to chat.

I eventually went to the supermarket out of desperation. I hated to go food shopping, but there was nothing left to eat in the house. Much to my dismay, I ran into Mrs. Bloch, a total busybody. I knew she'd want to talk about Mom and I really didn't want to.

"Claudia, how *are* you doing? Such a shame about your mother."

"It was inevitable. She'd been sick for so long."

"Poor woman suffered so."

"She's at peace now," I said, wishing the damn busybody would give me some peace.

She was about to say something else when she noticed another woman she knew passed. I'd just caught a lucky break.

"Oh, there's Beverly Watson. You do take care now and if you need anything, call," she said, practically running from me in order to catch up to the other woman. "Oh, Beverly... yoohoo... wait..."

Watching the short, pudgy little woman scamper away made me chuckle. She hadn't even given me the chance to thank her for her concern. In her own weird way, I knew she meant well. My mother had known her for years. I just didn't have the patience for her or the constant parade of people who often cornered me much in the same way. I needed a change of scenery—a vacation, perhaps. Then ultimately, maybe I would move to another place where I could start a new chapter in my life.

The next day I drove to the nearest travel agent. I had no idea where I wanted to go. I hadn't gone away or had any relaxation for such a long time that I couldn't remember where I vacationed last. The final few years were the worst, especially after Mom had been diagnosed with cancer. Originally the doctors were confident they had caught the disease in time to contain it. And for a while, it looked as if they had been right. Then, suddenly without warning, the nightmare started again. This time the cancer spread quickly. Mom deteriorated rapidly and her quality of life had been reduced to constant pain and suffering.

I found myself standing in front of a rack of brochures. All the travel agents were busy, so I began to browse through some of them.

"May I help you?" a pleasant voice behind me asked.

"I'm not sure. I'd like to take a vacation, but I have no idea where I want to go.

"Cruises are very popular this time of year. You can go to so many different places."

"I'd be going alone..."

"Single persons go on cruises all the time. It's a great way to meet people."

"It's a thought..."

"Have you ever been to the Caribbean?"

"No."

"That's a nice 7-day cruise. Here's the itinerary for a couple of cruise lines that go there."

I briefly looked through them and they both sounded great and very exciting. After what I had been doing for the last few years, most anything would sound exciting, though. I picked one.

"You're going to love this cruise," the travel agent said, as she keyed the information into the computer.

"I need to get away and relax."

"There's nothing more relaxing than a cruise. I go on one every year."

I paid for the trip, got a confirmation and left. The next few days were spent on buying clothes to wear on the cruise. The prospect of meeting men both scared and excited me. I couldn't remember the last time I'd even been on a date.

***

I arrived at the Port of Miami with a little time to spare. I found the ship I would be cruising on and was glad it bore no resemblance to the Titanic—or the Poseidon—not that I was superstitious, or anything. I got on the end of the line and watched as the people ahead of me boarded. They were of all ages and some had families. I guess I was automatically scanning the crowd for those men in my age bracket, the middle thirties, and early forties. Deep in my heart, I knew I was running out of time to marry and have children. And honestly, I didn't want to spend the rest of my life alone.

Looking at all the couples, I began to get cold feet, wondering why I'd come by myself in the first place. I should have asked a friend to accompany me. But whom? Most of my friends from college were married. The single ones had their own agendas. When my mother took her turn for the worse, I practically dropped out of life, in order to care for her.

I had boarded the ship. There was no turning back now. All I had to do now was convince myself I was going to have a wonderful time. Perhaps I'd even meet a guy...

"Hello, Ms. Rybeck. Welcome aboard!" a good-looking young man in a uniform greeted me.

"Thank you," I said and shook his hand. What is it about uniforms? They made men look so attractive in them, I thought as I went in search of my cabin. The ship was tremendous; elevators and stairs were available leading to countless decks. We were preparing to sail soon and the bon voyage parties were winding down. I passed an open stateroom where such a party was breaking up.

"Have a terrific time, Blake. Meet a beautiful woman."

"That's what I'm here for, Sis, right?"

The woman didn't answer the handsome man's sarcasm. He was by far the most attractive man I had encountered thus far.

I walked a little further and found my cabin in the next corridor. It was a small stateroom with two double beds. The cost difference between the cabin I was in and a smaller one was minuscule. I wanted to be comfortable, so I pulled out all the stops. My luggage was already there, waiting for me. I began to unpack. The ship's horn blared notifying all guests to disembark.

I locked my cabin and rode the elevator to the main deck where I could watch the boat set sail. Everyone was throwing out streamers and waving. It was a noisy, happy time. For the moment, I wished that I'd someone to wave to. With a sigh, I pushed the depressing thought from my mind. After all, wasn't I here to have a good time?

"Excuse me," a man said, interrupting my thoughts, "would you be so kind and snap our picture?"

He was a timid looking little man with a mousy-looking wife. He had a slight accent. I judged it to be Midwestern in origin. They made a cute couple in their matching Bermuda shorts. I was delighted to take their picture.

"Thank you so much," the man said as I handed back his camera.

I eventually found my way back to my cabin, hoping to see the handsome man again. His stateroom door was closed, so I walked on.

I had chosen the early seating for dinner. My table was comprised of all single people, six, counting myself. As usual, there were more women than men, though one of the men acted more like a woman with his incessant chatter. Of course, I'd hoped the handsome man I'd seen earlier would have been seated at my table. But after scanning the dining room and not seeing him, I surmised he must have chosen to dine at the second sitting.

The incessant talker spoke about topics I'd the least interest in. I wasn't alone in my thoughts, for the others looked just as bored. Everyone, being polite, let him drone on. I thought he resembled a barrel. His beige leisure suit added credence to the image. He continually emphasized what he was saying with his hands and knocked over the salt shaker twice. The only other man sat on my left. From the expression on his face, I could see the barrel-like man was a distraction to him as well.

"He'll sleep well tonight," he whispered to me.

I chuckled. "My name is Claudia Rybeck."

"Steve Meyers. Man, he sure can talk."

"Giving new meaning to the old saying, 'Talk is cheap.'"

Steve laughed. He had black hair and brown eyes that twinkled when he laughed. He

seemed pleasant enough, even if he wasn't as handsome as the man I had seen earlier. I realized right then and there that I wouldn't be happy until I met that other man. But, I feared I wasn't glamorous or rich enough to attract such a man. I was average in looks and height. Nothing special.

Steve interrupted my thoughts. "Where are you from?"

"Florida. Jupiter, actually."

"I wouldn't have guessed. You're not bronzed like most people who live in such a sunny climate."

"I'm unfortunately allergic to the sun. With my fair skin coloring, I must be careful. I moved to Florida to be with my mother when my father died."

"I'm from Massachusetts, but I go to Florida often to visit my parents who live in West Palm."

We talked as we ate. I did get to meet the others at the table eventually. The talkative man turned out to be a CEO from some big computer company out west. This kept the two sisters sitting closest to him interested. They were from Chicago and had retired from the real estate business. The other woman was a secretary from Omaha and was recently divorced. She made it more than obvious that she intended to go home with a trophy on her arm. Personally, I thought she'd be better off chilling for some time after a divorce. A person could get hurt jumping from the frying pan into the fire. But I was probably not the best person to give advice concerning marriage and divorce since I hadn't experienced either.

Steve seemed to be a nice guy, but he did nothing for me. He was a lawyer from some prestigious-sounding law firm in Massachusetts, but I wasn't going to let money blind me. It could only cover the flaws in the person cosmetically. I guess I still wanted love to be the motivating factor in my relationships. I was such a romantic that I still expected to hear bells and whistles go off when I met the right guy. I gave up looking for the white knight to come galloping in on his trusty steed ages ago, though.

After dinner, I took a walk around the ship. I'd feared Steve would ask to accompany me, but he didn't. There was something very depressing about him and I didn't want to get wet from the dark cloud that hovered above him. What I needed was sunshine. I'd had my fill of rain.

It was a beautiful night. The ship was lighted like a Christmas tree and the sky was studded with a blanket of shimmering stars. I watched from the deck as the ship smoothly sliced through the dark water.

"Beautiful night isn't it?" a deep voice said behind me.

I turned to face the handsome stranger from earlier. My heart began to bang against my chest. I suddenly felt like a young schoolgirl.

"Yes, yes, it is."

"Do you mind if I join you?"

"Please do."

"My name is Blake Henry, and I'm from Georgia," he drawled.

"Claudia Rybeck, from Florida," I said, extending my hand.

The touch of his hand on mine sent goosebumps down my arm. In the light I could see his eyes were green. His hair was close to my own color, a strawberry blond. If his eyes had been blue like mine, we probably could pass for close relatives. I didn't think I could ever tire of looking into those gorgeous eyes.

He interrupted my thoughts. "Is this your first cruise or do you do this often?"

"My maiden voyage."

"Me, too. My sister talked me into coming. 'Time to get on with your life,' she said."

I put a sympathetic look on my face, yet I couldn't find the words to ask what he was recovering from. Perhaps he guessed my thoughts.

"My wife was killed in a freak skiing accident on our honeymoon."

"Oh, how awful. I'm so sorry."

"According to my sister, three years is long enough to grieve."

"I don't think you can fit grief into a time frame. Everyone is different."

"I agree, but in my case, perhaps she's right."

"Only you can decide that. No one can force you to seek happiness."

"Wise words from such an attractive lady. What brings you on this cruise?"

"I needed to get away on a relaxing vacation. My mother recently passed away from a long bout with cancer."

"Now I know where the wisdom comes from. I'm sorry to hear about your loss."

"It's not as devastating as losing a wife, but it can be just as debilitating."

"I noticed there are no rings on your fingers. I take it you're not married."

"No."

"Good. I've always feared conversing with a woman only to have some crazed man come charging after me demanding satisfaction."

The image made me chuckle. "To defend their honor of course. Have no fear; no one is going to come after you. You have my solemn promise."

We made plans to have lunch together the day after tomorrow when we disembarked in Mexico and breakfast tomorrow. I truly hoped that it was only the first of many.

"Oh, there you are!" a high-pitched, feminine voice called out, obviously not intended for me.

"Oh, hello, Abigail. Abigail sits at my table. Claudia, Abigail. Abigail, Claudia."

If looks could kill, I'd be dead. The woman was decked in what looked like expensive jewelry. I was surprised she could manage to lift her arms in order to wave. She was a walking meal ticket for some money-hungry man. I couldn't help myself from disliking her, especially because of her intrusion. From the moment she got there, she dominated the conversation and made me feel most uncomfortable. Finally, I excused myself and left. The only shred of dignity that I was able to carry away with me was Blake's reminder about our plans for breakfast tomorrow and lunch in Cozumel.

As I walked away, I heard her say in a voice dripping with sarcasm, "I hope I *didn't* scare her away."

As if that hadn't her very intention. If Blake were interested in money, there would be no contest. The only thing I had to offer was love.

I passed Steve and waved. He nodded. He was talking to a woman and seemed content. I felt tired and headed back towards my cabin. As I undressed, I thought about Blake. Perhaps I shouldn't have left him in that woman's clutches. But I knew, what will be, will be. I strongly believed in fate.

Blake met me in the dining room the following morning. We decided to have our breakfast on the deck. I looked around, but Abigail wasn't in sight. Perhaps she wasn't an early riser. Or maybe it took a great deal of time for her to put on her makeup and jewelry. I was well aware how catty I was being. However, I didn't care.

He was such a charming man, the kind any woman would desire to be with. I especially admired his ability to discuss any subject. It turned out that we had a great deal in common. Even though he had eventually gone into the family business, originally Blake had wanted to teach history. Unfortunately, he never became an educator as I had. Instead, Blake's father had begun a car dealership in Atlanta. One dealership grew into a second and then a third. Before long, he had a chain throughout greater Atlanta. His father coaxed him into coming into the business and that was the end of his notion of a teaching career. It would seem he was quite a wealthy man in his own right. No wonder Abigail was after him.

Since we'd be at sea the entire day, we took advantage of the entertainment the ship offered. Between the sumptuous spreads of food and drink, the hours seemed to melt away. However, it was the company that made my heart better faster. However, I was always on guard to hear Abigail's annoying voice interrupt us. Luckily, it didn't happen until after dinner in the ship's casino. I didn't care. Blake and I had already made plans for the following day in Cozumel.

We spent the day together, touring the Mexican ruins. Since I'd remembered to bring my camera, I had a man take our picture together. Blake bought me a little keepsake, an inexpensive ring, to remember our day together. That was such a sweet thing to do. I was having a terrific time with this wonderful man; I'd hoped the day would never end. We had dinner on shore and saw a show including lively Flamenco dancing and a very loud Mariachi band. Eventually, it became time to head back to the boat.

Blake invited me to join him in a nightcap. As we walked into the main lobby of the ship, a dark cloud in the form of Abigail Arnold appeared. "There you are!" she called, looking directly at Blake. She had a way of making me feel invisible.

Dressed in a clinging black satin dress which shimmered in the light as she moved if you tried hard enough you could hear her jewelry clink as she walked. Funny how her every move whispered money.

Blake seemed to be too much of a gentleman to shoo her away and invited her to join us, an invitation she too quickly accepted. So much for possible romancing between Blake and me. There was no way for me to make this woman uncomfortable. She was oblivious to my very presence. I felt obligated to stay and have one drink before going back to my cabin. Being in Abigail's presence was quite insufferable.

I sipped some of my drink and pleaded exhaustion.

"Understandably after the day, we spent ashore. Get some rest, dear, and I'll see you tomorrow," Blake said as he gave me a chaste kiss good night.

I walked back to my cabin furious. Furious at myself for being a coward, furious at

Abigail for being a relentless thorn in my side, and furious at Blake for being the gentlemen he was and not sending her packing. It took quite a while before I eventually fell into an exhausted sleep.

It seemed that Abigail was dogging my path. As a female canine, she was able to stiff us out, no matter where we went. And each time Blake welcomed her. It finally dawned on me that he liked having the attention of two women. Perhaps he even envisioned us coming to blows over him. Well, he was dead wrong if he thought anything like that. I had no intention of ever fighting over a man. Or maybe I didn't think I had a chance of winning. Whatever, I decided not to try. At that point, I began to back off gracefully. By the end of the cruise, I doubted if either Blake or Abigail realized I wasn't around. Perhaps they were meant for each other. Of course, it bothered me a great deal at first, but the cruise was nearly over, and I wanted to leave with pleasant memories. So, I tried to have a good time despite the two of them.

*** 

I'm a firm believer that things always happen for the best. A month after I returned from my cruise, I met a nice guy at the college. He had replaced the Dean of Students who had left for greener pastures. Charles Roberson wasn't a flashy guy like Blake, but he was sweet and could light up any room when he smiled. We also had a great deal more in common than Blake and I ever did.

I never thought I'd ever find a man who'd love me for merely being myself. Charles always listened to what I had to say as if it were gospel, hanging onto my every word, making me feel important. He wasn't handsome in a classic way, as Blake had been, but he was the most handsome man in the world to me. I could never tire gazing into those soft brown eyes any more than I could become bored kissing his sweet lips. Nor was he wealthy, being an academic like me. He was a comfortable kind of guy and we fit together with ease.

I had never thought men had the same fears as women. I guess, ultimately, nobody wants to end up alone. One night when we both had a little too much wine with dinner, I discovered Charles was more like me than I'd ever imagined.

"Claudia, I love you."

"I know, Charles. I love you, too."

"I can't believe how lucky I am."

I thought he was getting maudlin from the wine. Actually, he was opening up and speaking what was on his mind.

"We're both lucky to have found each other."

"I just never thought I'd ever find a woman who'd want a guy like me."

"And what's wrong with you?"

"You know..."

"No, I really don't. I think you're wonderful."

"You're prejudiced."

"And what if I am?"

"Then you can't see."

"See what?"

"I'm a geek—a nerd."

"A cute one at that."

"You're making this a joke."

"No. I just think you're being silly putting yourself down."

"No. I'm merely being honest."

"Well, if it's honesty you're looking for; I have a confession to make as well. I didn't think there was a man out here for me...one who'd want me just as I am."

"An attractive woman like you? No, I don't believe that."

"I guess it works both ways."

"Then we're just the luckiest people in the world," Charles said, kissing my palm.

"I'll have to agree," I said drawing him closer so I could kiss him.

The kiss became long and more passionate, heating the warmth that had been simmering within me. I saw the desire in his eyes and felt it in his touch. I took his hand and led him into my bedroom. We made love, which was tender and sweet. Whenever I was nestled in his arms, I found a safe haven and forgot the world outside.

***

Months passed and my Caribbean cruise had been relegated to mere pictures in a photo book. Charles and I'd grown closer and were soon speaking of marriage. It wasn't a question of if we'd be getting married, but when. I was also back at the college teaching full time and doing research for a new curriculum I was developing for the following year. This chapter of my life was a happy one and boasted a long future.

***

One Sunday morning, we were at my apartment having brunch and reading the newspaper as we normally did. Charles had his head buried inside the main news section, while I started perusing the local news section.

"Claudia, what is it? You're as white as a sheet?"

"This news article... I...can't believe it."

He took the paper from my trembling hands and began to read aloud. "The new marriage of Blake and Abigail Henry was cut short when Mrs. Henry was killed in an automobile accident on Friday. The police impounded the car for an inspection. The Henrys were residents of West Palm Beach, where Mrs. Henry, along-time resident, had owned a villa." He thought for a moment and then asked, "Weren't they the people who were on the cruise with you?"

"Yes, Blake was the handsome man I told you about and Abigail was the woman with all the jewelry."

"Death like this is so tragic, but when you know the person involved, it makes the loss more upsetting."

"I didn't like Abigail. She had intruded on my time too much, but I do feel bad about her death. But..."

"What?"

"Something worries me..."

"What's wrong?"

"Blake had told me he'd lost another bride on a honeymoon accident about four years ago. Can a man be so unlucky in love?"

"Perhaps..."

"Or perhaps, not."

"What are you intimating?" Charles asked.

"Could there be others?"

"Like women? Claudia, what are you suggesting?"

"What if someone had tampered with the car and it wasn't an accident? What if Blake has done this before? Maybe his other wife who had been killed in a skiing accident, had really been pushed off a cliff?"

"You're making the man sound like a serial killer."

"If he is, somebody else is going to die."

"Good Lord, Claudia! Do you realize what you're saying?"

"However, then again...it doesn't make sense. I remember Blake as being such a charming man."

"So was Ted Bundy," he replied, verbally splashing cold water in my face.

"But Charles, on the other hand, don't you think if there were any suspicion the authorities would have picked up on it? I mean, the man could really have lousy luck in love, you know."

"I know you'd like to believe that, but I don't believe in coincidence."

"So why didn't the authorities get suspicious?" I asked again.

"Sometimes it isn't so easy to put two and two together. What if something else important happened at the same time he allegedly did away with the women? Or better still, what if he moved a great deal and changed his name?"

"But he told me his father owned a chain of auto dealerships—"

"What if everything he told you were lies and he was only on the cruise looking for rich women? He did choose Abigail over you, didn't he?" Charles said.

Suddenly I began to get a totally different image of Blake Henry. Maybe he was after Abigail all along and used me to make *her* jealous. Hey, if he did this for a living, he'd become pretty good at it. They say the first time you commit a crime is always the hardest. After that, it's a piece of cake. Running with that premise, Blake Henry, or whoever the hell he was, was going to seek out another woman of means and kill her. Could I just forget about this, knowing what I already know?

"Maybe I should check out Blake Henry's background and go to the authorities."

"You'll do no such thing. Sweetheart, you're not an investigative reporter. Besides, you have that new curriculum to devise."

"And?"

"Aside from the fact you can't neglect me, don't forget that curiosity killed the cat."

I was so bothered by the thought that Blake Henry could be a murderous fortune-seeker I could hardly sleep that night. Why was I so concerned, ignoring Charles's good advice? The only answer I could come up with after soul-searching was the fact Blake Henry had come on to me first. Had Abigail not been on that cruise, would I be alive today? After all, he knew my mother had just passed away. He could have thought I might have been left a large inheritance. However, if my suspicions about Blake Henry were true, if he only married women of wealth and killed them, how could I merely close my eyes and allow him to get away with it?

Every nerve in my body told me to forget about Blake and what he might or might not have done, but the inquisitive investigative side of my nature told me differently. I knew where there was smoke, there was usually a fire simmering. Was there one in Blake's case? Contrary to what he'd told me, I got the feeling that Charles was right, and Blake most likely moved around a great deal. Perhaps this is what made it difficult for the authorities to link his crimes.

I remembered reading in the news article that the couple was living in West Palm Beach in a villa formerly owned by Mrs. Henry. It would seem that he'd kept her alive long enough for her to amend her will. On the cruise she'd spoken of her children having been married and well taken care of.

Slow down, lady, I cautioned myself. All this is conjecture. None of it may be true. But I knew I'd never rest until I knew the truth.

It's very hard to remain anonymous in today's technological age. Everything we do always seems to leave a paper trail. I spent a few hours a day delving into Blake Henry's background. Having a friend in the police department was a tremendous help.

John Seever and I were childhood friends. As kids, he always played the cop and I got to be the robber whom he arrested. When I called John and asked for his help, he agreed to, but only up to a point. We couldn't do anything which would attract attention. I gave him Blake's picture and the information I knew about him. He'd try and find out if he'd been in any legal trouble and trace whatever licenses he had. It would give us an idea of his travels.

I would check the major newspapers for back-stories and society weddings. If Blake had been married before, I'd find out. Name changes weren't usually a problem. They merely slowed things down. Computers were such wonderful research tools.

***

Charles came behind my chair and nuzzled my neck. I guess the program he'd been watching on TV was over.

"Hi, sweetheart. Bored?"

"Since you've been researching public enemy number 1, you have to ask?"

I closed down the computer. "I'm sorry. I didn't mean to neglect you," I said, grabbing his hand and kissing it.

"I love you, but it's hard to compete with an obsession."

"I'm not obsessed."

"Then what are you? Driven?"

"It's just that I'm staring at the tip of the iceberg here. I know Blake's been married at least one other time. She died also, except hers might have been a natural death."

"And if you discover he has married a number of times before and his wives all met untimely ends, what will you do then?"

"Turn my information over to the authorities and hopefully they will eventually arrest and prosecute him."

He looked at me with a worried expression on his face, as if he didn't believe that it would end there.

"I don't want anything to happen to you. I love you."

"Stop being so paranoid. Nothing will happen to me. I love you too much to let someone else have you," I said.

I got up and kissed his lips. He took my face in his hands and looked into my eyes as if he were memorizing it. Then he kissed my eyes, my face, and my mouth. We walked into the bedroom and made sweet love. I loved Charles with all my heart and never wanted to give him a moment's worry. From now on, I wouldn't do any research on Blake Henry when he was around. That way I wouldn't upset him.

With the help of my police friend, I had pieced together quite a dossier on Blake Henry, who also used the name Barry Henderson while he was residing in Seattle. He had been married eight times in twelve years, living in almost as many states. None of his wives survived to live for more than a year with him. He was definitely a sociopath who married women for their money and then rigged their deaths to make them look like accidents. Nothing that Blake had said was true. He didn't come from Georgia and his father hadn't been a businessman. Instead, his father had been a drunkard with a penchant for prostitutes. He died when Blake was sixteen from an ulcerated liver. They were living in Arkansas at the time, though Blake had been born in Mississippi. There were no car dealerships belonging to Blake's father. Blake had invested as a silent partner in one while he was living in Georgia, but it failed.

Since the crimes took place in several states, John told me to bring the evidence to the FBI. Not wanting to see any more women killed, I got in touch with them immediately. Blake Henry, or whatever name he went by now, was definitely a monster. I thanked my lucky stars for not getting involved with him. That handsome face was only a mask hiding the pure evil that lies beneath.

Charles was thrilled to know I'd finally put my investigation of Blake Henry to rest. I'd proven what I'd originally set out to do and by doing so, would probably save lives as well. Of course, the fact that I'd come out unscathed was what mattered the most to him.

***

I was meeting Charles for dinner on his birthday at our favorite restaurant. I got there first and parked. As I locked the car, someone grabbed me from behind. I struggled to get away from him. It hadn't occurred to me that my attacker might have a gun or knife. I was too busy protecting Charles' birthday present in my purse.

"Hey, you! Get away from her!" Charles shouted as he charged over to my aid.

It startled my attacker and he ran off. I fell into Charles' arms.

"Are you okay, baby?"

"I...I...think so."

"Do you want to go home?"

"And spoil your birthday dinner? No way."

"We can do it again some other time."

I shook my head. "Just give me a few moments to catch my breath. I'm all right."

"Did you see his face?"

"No. Probably some kid who needed money for drugs."

"You're probably right," he said staring off in the direction my attacked fled.

"Are you sure you're okay?" Charles asked again.

"Yes. Let's go inside. I think I need to sit down."

We went into the restaurant. I was determined to pull myself together. I didn't want to spoil Charles' birthday celebration. Somehow, I even forced myself to eat much of what I'd ordered. The two drinks I'd downed beforehand helped a great deal in calming my frayed nerves, as well.

By the time we headed back to my place, the attempted mugging was on its way to becoming history. All I wanted to do was lie in Charles' arms and make love with him, which is exactly what we did.

In the afterglow of our lovemaking, Charles thanked me again for his gold watch. I knew he'd love just about anything I got him, but the watch was practical since his watch was constantly at the jeweler's being fixed.

We fell asleep wrapped in each other's arms.

***

I didn't see much of Charles in the next few days. A new semester was starting and being the Dean of Students, he had to prepare for it.

I would be eating alone tonight. At first, Charles thought he'd be able to get away early and have dinner with me, but at the last minute he had to cancel. I was tired, anyway, and decided to have a light meal and go to bed early.

The traffic that evening had been horrendous, and it took longer than usual to get home. I decided on a quick shower to perk me up since I feared falling asleep in a bath. I got my mail and went into the house. It suddenly seemed so oppressively quiet, so I turned on the small TV in the kitchen to keep me company while I sifted through the mail, throwing away the junk. The news was on, but I paid little attention. I put the new bills that had just come in on the stack with the older ones. I made a mental note to take some time out this weekend to pay them.

I walked into my bedroom and sat down on the bed to take my shoes off. My feet were tired from having been on them a great deal today. I'd used the blackboard and overhead projector for much of my lectures. Absentmindedly I rubbed them, thinking of the lectures I was giving tomorrow to my other classes. I sighed and began to undress when the phone began to ring.

"Hello?"

"Thought I'd give you a quick call. Miss you."

"Miss you, too, love," I replied.

"We'll meet for dinner after your last class tomorrow."

"The usual place?" I asked, thinking of the small dinner we often went to during the week.

"No. How about Chinese, for a change?" he suggested.

"Sounds good. The restaurant on fifteenth?"

"Sure, why not. Love you."

"Love you, too," I said, replacing the receiver.

Suddenly, I felt a hand roughly slide across my face to cover my mouth and a sharp point at my throat. I couldn't have made any noise had I'd wanted to, anyway. My throat had been sucked bone-dry by fear.

"Hello, my dear. It's been a while."

I recognized the smooth voice as belonging to Blake Henry. The fear transformed into terror. "Blake! What are you doing here?"

"Funny you should ask."

"Why?" I asked, trying to keep my voice steady. It seemed a stupid thing to try and do when I was visibly trembling, on the verge of losing it entirely.

"Don't play stupid with me. I, too, have a friend in law enforcement."

He knew. I was just as good as dead. My insides had been reduced to pure jelly now.

"You're a lucky woman, but your luck has run out. And so, has my patience."

I nearly collapsed, but he pulled me up. It would have been easy the other night, a mugging gone bad. But your Mr. Wonderful had to come along and interrupt."

"It was *you* the other night in the parking lot?"

"None other."

"You've been following me?"

"For quite a while now. Now let's get this over with. I have a date."

"What are you going to do with me?"

"Give you the accident of your life," he said, laughing at his own joke.

I was so glad he thought it was funny. Here I was, not knowing when I'd be taking my last breath, and he was enjoying himself. Delay was my only tactic. If I could get to the phone, I could call for help.

I'd forgotten I was in my underwear, which was lacy and sheer until I realized he was looking at my breasts. Instinctively, I covered my chest. He pulled my arms down. A smirk had formed on his face.

"You know, I truly liked you, Claudia," he said, running his hand gently down the side of my face.

I felt myself go numb inside and yet I tried not to show it and cringe. I didn't want the mood to change. Yet, with a sociopath, it probably wouldn't matter.

"You were so much more attractive than Abigail. Her body wasn't nearly as nice. Sleeping with her was such a chore," he said, grazing the tops of my breasts with his fingertips.

"I liked you, too. I was upset that you kept allowing Abigail to join us."

"True, we never had the chance to be alone and explore the possibilities."

A million scenarios began to run through my mind. If I got him to have sex with me, how would he do it? Leave his pants on, take them off, or lower them? I needed a few seconds to get out of here and get into my office. It had a lock and I could dial 911. The thought of having sex with the monster was horrible, but the alternative was much worse.

"We have all the time in the world now," I said, tracing his lips with my finger, hoping I sounded enticing enough.

He smiled. "You're right. You still want me, don't you?"

"More than anything," I said breathlessly.

I had never played a vixen in my life, but I was going to have to give an award-winning role if I wanted to see another day. This man obviously had an ego the size of Montana and responded well to flattery

I lay back on the bed and drew him towards me. Luckily, he was more interested in kissing my body than my mouth. He quickly freed my breasts and greedily feasted on them. I moaned to let him think I was getting aroused. That seemed to please him, and he began to explore the rest of me with his hands. I could see he was already aroused, so I began to fumble with the zipper on his slacks, hoping he'd get the message and pull them down. That way, if he tried to chase me, he'd trip over them.

"You really want this, don't you? All you women are the same," he spat, as he got off the bed and began to take off his slacks. When they reached the point below his knees, I pushed him over backward and ran from the room.

"You bitch!" he screamed and tripped as he instinctively tried to run after me.

I'd just bought myself a few seconds as I ran into my office and locked the door. Grabbing the phone, I dialed 911. Seconds later, the door was shattered and Blake stormed in. I dropped the phone to the floor in fright and began to back away.

"Nice move, bitch, but the game's over and you lose," he said as he reached for me.

I was able to slip from his grasp for the moment and put my hand down on something cold and hard which was lying on the desk. I recognized its engraving. It was my dad's ornate letter opener, the one my mother begged him to hide in the drawer when I was small, so I wouldn't play with it and hurt myself.

"It's time to go nightie-night, Claudia—permanently," he said as he roughly grabbed me.

I plunged the letter opener into his chest. He screamed. I plunged it again and again. Blood spurted everywhere. He fell to his knees. Like a crazy woman, I kept stabbing him, until he stopped moving. Finally, I realized what I had done and dropped the letter opener and began to scream. I'd come completely undone.

When the police came rushing in, they found me in the same spot, my throat raw from screaming.

"Are you okay, ma'am?"

I looked up with vacant eyes. I wasn't certain of anything. Finally, the shock wore off and I nodded. An officer put a blanket around me and led me from the room, as another picked the phone from the floor and replaced it in its cradle.

"Is there someone you'd like us to call?"

I gave them Charles' number. He was still in the office, finishing up for the night.

"Tell her I'll be right there!" He said it so loudly that I was able to hear him.

They were taking pictures of the crime scene. I tried to them, as coherently as I was able to at that point, what had happened. I might have had a blanket around me, but there was a chill within me that nothing could warm.

Charles came rushing in as the coroner was removing Blake's body. I collapsed in his strong, safe arms. Suddenly the tears came streaming out. I'd fallen apart again.

"It's okay now, baby, I'm here."

"You were right. I should have listened to you," I whispered between sniffles.

"It's over. Shhh!"

Charles rocked and held me until the shakes passed. By that time the police were ready to leave. Charles helped me gather what I'd need to wear tomorrow and took me to his place. I was more than glad to leave my house. I doubted if I'd ever feel safe living there again.

We took a shower together and Charles helped me wash all the dry, encrusted blood from my hair and body. I was glad he was with me; I didn't want to be alone for a minute.

After the shower, Charles made omelets. I ate, hardly tasting the food. Having something warm in my stomach didn't hurt. What I needed most of all was to be held. Charles realized this and we got into bed early. I knew he'd had a long day and was most likely exhausted, but he was more concerned with comforting me. A big reason for loving this caring man.

As I lay safely nestled in his arms, I became cognizant of the fact that I was probably one of the luckiest women alive. Just being alive was the most wonderful part. Of course, finding a man like Charles was the other important aspect. I intended to give him the best of my love for the rest of my life. I had no idea what life held in store for me, but there would always be a place in it for Charles.

THE END

# MARRIED TO A STRANGER
By Candace Gold

The night I told Paul I was pregnant was the most romantic one of my life. We were celebrating our third anniversary. Paul had hired a limo to pick us up at our apartment and take us to the Galaxy, the glitzy new hotel in town. There we dined and danced half the night away. A dozen long-stemmed roses were waiting upstairs in our suite on the fourteenth floor overlooking the city. And what a breath-taking view it was.

I'd been waiting for just the right moment to tell Paul we were going to have a baby. I knew how much he wanted one. He'd look at all the babies in the strollers we passed and would often stop while we were shopping to show me the bat and glove he was going to buy for his son. Or the free-standing basketball hoop, so they could play one-on-one. He'd ramble on about how he intended to be the best father a kid could have. He'd never be the kind his own father was, neglectful and abusive.

We'd just made love in the huge round bed and were lying in the afterglow as our vitals returned to normal. Paul was on his side facing me, drawing lazy circles around one of my nipples with his finger. In my heart, I felt it was time.

"Sweetheart, there's something I have to tell you," I said, finally breaking the news.

"What?"

"I'm pregnant."

"That's nice, Marisa...What did you say?"

"I'm going to have a baby."

Paul shot up like a rocket to a sitting position and grabbed me by my shoulders so he could look directly into my eyes. "You really are, right? I mean, this isn't a joke or something."

I nodded, beaming with joy knowing that I was able to grant the man I loved his biggest wish. "No joke. You really are going to be a father."

"That's wonderful, baby," he said and kissed me.

Then he lightly touched my still flat belly and asked, "When?"

"I held up eight fingers."

Paul was beside himself with happiness and started to make plans for his son. He was so sure it was going to be a boy. I hoped it turned out to be a boy, too. I didn't want him to be disappointed.

***

I had an easy pregnancy. I didn't get morning sickness even once. When I finally went into labor Paul was a nervous wreck. I had my doubts about ever getting to the hospital in one piece before the baby arrived. Paul must have broken every traffic law on the books, fearing that he wouldn't get me there on time.

Little Paul Martin, Jr. was the most beautiful baby in the entire world. He had my black hair, his father's blue eyes, and the lungs of a giant. I counted all his fingers and toes, glad that he was healthy. Now we were a perfect family and I felt blessed.

The first few weeks after we brought Paul Jr. home Paul tried to be a good father. He'd even get up sometimes at night to feed the baby and change his diaper. When he came home from work, he'd kiss me and hurry in to see little Paul. Just seeing the two of them together brought tears of joy to my eyes. We seemed to be the ideal family. But all that soon changed...

The baby's crying began to give him headaches. Paul would be annoyed with me when I didn't drop everything and rush into the living room to be with him—even if it was only to watch some silly sitcom on TV. He always seemed to want to do things when it was time to care for Paul Jr. Everything I did or didn't do began to irritate him. He complained bitterly how the baby ruined our lives. We couldn't just pick-up and go away, anymore. Nor could we go out to a movie or dinner without first finding someone to watch the baby. To him, the baby had become something of a nuisance—an intrusion—ruining our lives.

Paul began to stay longer at the office. I'd get a call around 4:00 PM telling me not to expect him for dinner. He'd catch something outside. "Don't wait up," he'd say. "I might be late." At first, it was once in a while, but soon it became once or twice a week. Then Paul started to go away on business trips every other week. I didn't realize how much he was staying away until little Paul got very sick.

It began as a cold. But soon the baby was coughing. The deep-sounding hacking coming from someone so small frightened me. I was normally apprehensive being responsible for another life so dependent, but not knowing how to handle his condition terrified me. I took him to the doctor, but the medicine prescribed for the baby seemed to make his cough worse. I'd never been as frightened as I was then. I was all alone with no family or friends to turn to for help. Paul was away on one of his business trips and I had no idea where he was or when he was returning. Frantic, I called the doctor back and he told me to bring Paul Jr. in. I bundled up the baby and took him back to the doctor. On the way, I called Paul's cell phone but got his voice mail. I needed Paul and wanted him to come home, so I left a message.

The baby was now running a high fever, so the doctor gave him a shot and wrote another prescription to fill. If the fever didn't break, he instructed me to take the baby to the emergency room. The doctor's words echoed in my head. What if Paul Jr. worsened and died? I shook my head as if I could knock those horrible thoughts out of it.

Paul eventually returned my call about two hours later. I'll never forget what he said to me, for his words chilled my heart. Not even saying hello, he barked into the phone, "What the hell's so important that you had to have me call?"

"It's the baby—"

"It's *always* the baby."

"Paul, I don't want to argue. I need you. Paul's very sick."

"What do you expect *me* to do? Call a doctor, for God's sake."

"You don't understand—"

"Oh, yes I do. You'll see me when I get home!" Paul replied severing the connection.

I could hardly believe my own ears. What a *loving* father he had turned into. Better still, who *had* he become? I hadn't recognized the stranger I'd been speaking to on the phone.

Luckily the baby's fever finally broke. He began to get better. I'd been so petrified that I sat up and watched him sleep for two nights straight in order to make sure he was breathing. I did a great deal of thinking while I sat by Paul's crib. Having a child should come with a solemn vow like a marriage does. *To love in sickness and in health.* Infants have to depend on their parents to care for them. Having a baby isn't just playing ball and going to Disney World. It's a responsibility that should never be taken lightly. It's not like adopting a puppy and then returning it because you've discovered you don't like dogs.

By the time Paul returned home, I was both physically and mentally exhausted. He expected me to prepare his dinner and do his laundry immediately. Unfortunately, it happened to be feeding time for the baby and that came first. Paul had come home in a rotten mood and it steadily grew worse. He had zero tolerance for the baby and even less for me.

He continued to harp on the fact I gave more attention to the baby than him. What was wrong with him? Did he actually want me to forgo feeding Paul Jr. so I could play with him? I always made time for him—when he happened to be home, for a change. In fact, there was hardly a week that went by where Paul was home more than he was away. Plenty of times he'd come home late at night, smelling of alcohol, and wanting sex. As tired as I was, I never said no. I still loved him and tried to be a good wife. And that worked both ways. He could try to be a better husband.

I'll admit that Paul Jr. did take up a lot of my time, but he was an infant and couldn't fend for himself. Paul was a grown adult who was acting more like a jealous child. He felt that he had to compete with his own baby for my attention. His self-absorption and selfishness were beginning to get on my nerves. I eventually got annoyed and told him to stay home more. Then I'd pay more attention to him. Ultimately, things came to a terrible head...

***

Paul didn't take any business trips for an entire week. That in itself was a novelty. However, the fact that he would go to work, come home, have dinner, and plant himself in front of the TV the entire night waiting for me to go to sleep before he'd come to bed, threw my curiosity into a tailspin. Though I definitely thought his behavior was peculiar, I was willing to deal with it if it meant having him home. I also reasoned that he would tell me what was bothering him when he was ready. Whether or not I'd be prepared to hear it was another story entirely.

When the following Monday morning came, Paul packed his overnight bag and had a quick cup of coffee. I walked him to the door to say goodbye. As I was about to close it, he said, "I guess you're probably wondering why I was acting so weirdly this past week."

"I was. I figured you'd get around to telling me eventually."

"I thought I had gonorrhea and didn't want to give it to you."

I stood there stunned as if my brain was having difficulty trying to wrap itself around what he'd just said and its terrible implications. A moment later, when it had all registered, I slammed the door in his face. How could he stand there and tell me that? Didn't he think I'd react this way? Or did he think I was stupid enough to believe he caught it from a toilet seat? Or perhaps he didn't care what I thought?

Everything began to fall into place like the pieces of a puzzle. All the time Paul slept out he probably cheated on me. Maybe he even had a mistress. How could he do this to me? How could you hurt the woman you professed to love? Was he cheating because he no longer loved me? I suddenly felt so empty and miserable. However, most of all, I didn't know what to do. Perhaps I'd become too numb to think.

Paul called three days later. We ended up arguing over the phone. It had been over Paul Jr., as usual. He had wanted to meet me at a diner to talk. I told him Paul had just fallen asleep and I didn't want to wake him. That was all I said, but it was enough to ignite Paul's short fuse.

"Forget it!" he spat. "It's no use. I'll be home to pick up my things."

"What do you mean?"

"I'm leaving you."

"But where will you be staying?"

"That's none of your concern. I'll get in touch with you when it was time to sign the divorce papers."

Then he hung up. Okay, I shouldn't have been surprised about this since Paul hadn't been a good husband or father for so long, but even so, I was hardly prepared. I had no means of support. I didn't have a job. Therefore, I didn't have any viable way to pay the rent on the apartment or even buy food. I'd been totally dependent on Paul. I would have to find somebody to watch Paul Jr. in order to go back to work.

Things weren't as bleak as I first imagined. I couldn't afford a lawyer but thought maybe I wouldn't need one for Paul seemed to be playing fair by sending me money for the rent. I'd applied for food stamps and tried to find a good-paying job. The divorce papers hadn't been sent to me yet, so I thought that there was a slim chance he'd come to his senses and change his mind about getting one. In my mind, it was always better to try and rebuild rather than destroy. I hadn't truly worked out my feelings about him and felt so lost and alone.

Well, I was wrong about Paul. He was dead serious about the divorce and the papers arrived three weeks later. I was to receive alimony and child support. Between the two, I'd be able to just squeak by. To make things better, I needed a job that would pay enough to cover the cost of a babysitter for Paul Jr. But every time I'd try to actively look for one, the baby would get sick and I feared another experience like the one I had when he was an infant.

***

Six months later Paul called to offer me a deal. He would give me five thousand dollars if I gave him sole custody of Paul Jr. I couldn't believe my ears. He actually thought that I would sell my own child for five thousand dollars. But the fact that he wanted Paul Jr. all of a sudden, made his request sound bizarre. When I declined his offer, he got angry. He assured me that if I didn't give him the child voluntarily, he would sue me for custody and win.

I was terrified that he might win, and I would lose the one reason on earth that got me out of bed in the morning. Paul Jr. was my entire life. Since I had no visible means of support, all the cards were stacked in Paul's favor. I had to get legal advice. And that turned out to be easier said than done. Most lawyers wanted to be paid upfront and I had no money for a retainer.

After calling around, I finally ended in the law office of Theodore Silver. He was willing to listen to my problem without charging me. But the best part was that if he took my case, he would try to get Paul to pay for his services.

I was shown into Mr. Silver's office. A short, dark-haired man in a pinstriped gray suit rose from behind the desk to greet me.

"Welcome, Mrs. Martin. How can I be of service to you?"

"I need your help desperately. I don't even know where to begin?"

He smiled sympathetically. "I'm here to listen, so why not start at the beginning."

I took a deep breath in a vain attempt to steady my nerves. "My husband Paul and I just got divorced. And now he wants to take my child away from me." Despite my efforts not to, I began to cry.

"I see. Is he remarrying soon?"

"I don't know—he could be. He's been cheating on me ever since the baby was born."

"Can you prove any of this?"

I shook my head.

"Are you gainfully employed?"

"No. Paul has been sending me money. If he decided to stop, I'd have to go on welfare."

"Do you think he might stop sending you money?"

"With Paul anything is possible. He's definitely not the same person I married. He changed right after the baby was born. Ironically, he was the one who wanted to start a family in the first place. He wanted to be the best father he could—better than his own father had been. At first, he was happy with the baby, but soon he found Paul Jr. an annoyance and began to find excuses to stay away from home."

"If that be the case, why do you think Paul wants to sue you for sole child custody?"

"I don't know. I thought about this a great deal. The only viable reason I could come up with was that he was now with a woman who desired kids but couldn't conceive."

"That's as good as any theory at the moment. However, right now we have to concentrate on preventing him from getting Paul Jr."

"Then you'll help me?"

"Yes. I've always hated bullies and your ex-husband sounds like a nasty one."

"Oh, thank you." I had to restrain myself back from jumping on his desk and kissing him.

"Don't thank me yet. The way I see it, we are going to have an uphill battle if we don't do something to even up the sides."

"But, how can we do that?"

"Okay. Let's say for all intents and purposes, that I'm an *impartial* judge. I see before me a single woman with no visible means of support. I can also detect a slight accent. You came to this country as a child from an eastern European country."

I was amazed that he was so perceptive. "I was born in Hungary, but I'm a citizen."

"It shouldn't matter that you aren't a natural-born citizen, but it might subconsciously color the judge's verdict and another thing to keep in mind. Judges are only human, after all."

I looked down at my hands which were hardly still. I never thought my heritage might hurt me.

"Marisa—may I call you that?" he asked after realizing he'd become informal.

I nodded.

"I was only working up a possible scenario here. I want you to be aware of all the variables involved. I had no intention of making you feel worse than you already do."

"I understand."

"Okay, then. You're standing in front of the judge with no visible mean of support, while your ex-husband Paul, acting like the perfect father, has a wife, a home and a good job—the perfect scenario for a child to be brought up in."

"But he wasn't a good father, let alone a perfect one!"

"That's *your* side of the story. There are always two. Do you see where I'm heading with this?"

"Then, how could I possibly win." A tear slipped out of the corner of my eye and I wiped it away.

"Your chances are slim to none with the odds you now have. We've got to change that."

"But how?"

"You're getting married."

"What?" I didn't think I heard him correctly. With the dumb look I must have had on my face, I half-expected him to say, *what part of that sentence didn't you understand?*

He chuckled. "Sorry for the shock. What I intend to do, that is if you're agreeable, is to arrange a marriage of convenience for you. This will strengthen your position and hopefully help you to win the custody battle."

"But who... Who would marry me just like that? Is there a place you go to rent husbands? Then again, I wouldn't be surprised, we practically rent everything nowadays. My God, listen to me, I sound crazy."

He chuckled. "Sit down and let me finish explaining," he said.

I hadn't even realized I was standing, my head felt as if it had gotten caught in an emotional whirlwind. I didn't know how to feel at the moment. Should I be happy I was getting help, or apprehensive? What in the world had I gotten myself into? It was as if I walked through Alice's looking glass into Wonderland.

"After we win, I'll help you attain an annulment."

"But, who in the world am I going to marry?"

"Oh, yes, I'll get to that. But first, tell me if you're willing to do it."

I sat there dumbfounded. I never expected him to suggest marriage. However, if my getting married to a total stranger was going to help me beat Paul at his own game and help me keep Paul Jr., I'd do it. I'd do anything he suggested at this point.

"Well, what do you say?"

"Who would stick their neck out and agree to marry me?"

"That's no problem. *Will* you do it?"

I nodded, waiting to hear about my new *husband of convenience*.

"Good. I have a friend who lives in a large, empty house. Not only is he a very nice man, but he is also a very lonely man. An instant family might be the trick to cheer him up."

"But how do you know this man will want to marry me?"

"He owes me a favor."

"It must be a big one."

Mr. Silver smiled and asked if I had any questions before he started the ball rolling.

"Can you tell me something about your friend?"

"His name is Mark Robertson and he is in his late forties. He has two grown boys. Both are married and live in other states. His wife died many years ago from cancer."

"I get to live in his house and you're telling me he's not going to expect something in return from me?"

"I know where you're heading with that and the answer is absolutely not unless you want to."

"And he'll agree to that?"

"Definitely."

"But how can you be so sure?"

"I know Mark Robertson."

"When do I meet Mr. Robertson?"

"Hopefully today. Tomorrow, when you get married."

"Tomorrow!"

"Yes. And you better get used to calling him Mark. After all, you don't want the judge to think this was a marriage of convenience, do you?

I began to laugh when he said that.

"Good, I got you to laugh. Let me call Mark now. He's really a good guy and loves children."

I watched as Mr. Silver dialed Mark Robertson's number. Sitting there I thought about what I'd just agreed to do. I was going to marry a total stranger. I must be out of my mind. But

then, what would happen if I didn't and lost Paul Jr.? I shuddered at the thought. Did I want to take that chance? I resigned myself to the fact I had little choice and was doing the best thing possible. I couldn't afford to lose my son. He was my entire life now.

The phone call took less than ten minutes. Mark Robertson had agreed. In fact, he was on his way to meet me and Paul Jr. who was just outside with the receptionist. I began to panic. I must look like a mess. What if he didn't like me? What if I didn't like him? My face must have mirrored what I was thinking because Mr. Silver patted my hand. "Relax, Marisa. I promise you that everything was going to be fine."

*Yeah, and pigs can fly.*

"You and Mark will pick up a marriage license tomorrow morning and be married by a judge in the afternoon. A honeymoon is optional."

I can't tell you how strange I felt as I listened to the lawyer explain this to me. There was a discreet knock at the door. The receptionist brought Paul Jr. into Mr. Silver's office and said, "He's such a good baby. And so adorable."

She didn't have to tell me that. Paul Jr. was a wonderful baby and a joy.

Mark Robertson arrived a half-hour later. He walked in and went immediately to Paul Jr. In seconds, the baby was laughing. I took that as a good sign. I also began to breathe more easily. The fact that he didn't resemble the Hunchback of Notre Dame helped. I watched as he shook Mr. Silver's hand. Then he turned to face me. He took my hand and kissed it.

"Hello, beautiful lady. I hear you need a knight to be your champion. So how about we get married?"

I laughed. He seemed pleasant enough and had a sense of humor. "If you'll have me."

"It will be an honor. Now come. Our chariot awaits us. I'll take you to lunch and we'll get to know each other a little better. Then I'll show you and Paul where you're going to live."

He turned to Mr. Silver and said, "You don't like to lose, do you?"

Mr. Silver shook his hand and said, "Not in the slightest. And neither do you? Thank you, Mark." Then Mark gave Mr. Silver a hug. I guess they did know each other very well.

I thanked Mr. Silver and shook his hand also. Mine was still trembling and as he put his other hand over it, he said, "Everything will be fine, Marisa. You heard the man, I hate to lose."

I managed to give him a smile. Where had these two wonderful men come from? I was beginning to wonder if I had a guardian angel watching over me.

"I'll get in touch with the both of you when I get a court date," Mr. Silver said as we walked out.

Mark took us to a very nice restaurant. I later found out that he owned it. He also owned two more across town. As we talked, I studied him. He was an attractive man with salt-and-pepper hair. When he smiled, his entire face lit up and his blue eyes twinkled. He was also a good listener and tried to put me more at ease.

"May I ask you a question, Mark?"

"I can probably guess what it is. Sure, go ahead and ask."

"Why are you doing this? Why did you agree to marry a total stranger with a child, no less?"

"Simply because Ted Silver asked me to. We go back a long way. If it wasn't for Ted, I would have drowned in a bottle of scotch. When my wife died, he helped me get back on my feet so I could be a father to my kids. Now I can pay forward Ted's kindness by helping you stand up to your ex. After we win the custody battle, we could get the marriage annulled."

"I don't know how to thank you for your kindness."

"I haven't done anything yet. You can thank me *when* we win."

After lunch, we drove to his home. Mansion would be more like it. It was a huge place with an indoor pool and exercise room. He had a full-time housekeeper who served also as a cook. She lived in her own little cottage behind the house. Basically, he lived alone just as Ted Silver had said. The bedroom I slept in was separated from Paul's by an adjoining bathroom, which turned out to be one of four. I was quite thrilled I didn't have to clean the place or the four bathrooms.

We got married as planned. I moved into Mark's house that evening. He graciously stored the few pieces of furniture I cared about keeping in the basement of one of his restaurants. It was awkward at first, but I made believe I was staying at a resort on an endless vacation. Mark was semi-retired and was home a great deal. After being alone so much even when I was still married, having someone around to talk to who spoke in a language that wasn't gibberish was a pleasure. He also turned out to be good company. We went on picnics and did everything as if we were a real family. To someone who didn't know our situation, we were.

Mark was even willing to watch little Paul so I could have some time for myself. He bought me my own car so I could go places by myself if I wanted to. In fact, I was free to come and go as I desired. I couldn't believe how lucky I was to have such a kind and generous man to take care of me and not ask anything in return.

Mr. Silver said that our marriage wouldn't be put on trial, only my fitness as a mother. Even so, he still had Mark rehearse with me where we met and how long we'd known one another.

When Mr. Silver called to let us know when we had to appear in court, I was nervous, but knowing Mark would be there with me was comforting. People tell you never to count your chickens before they hatch. I now know why.

The first day in court wasn't too bad. There was only a judge to listen to our case and no jury. I wanted to fall through the floor when Paul walked into the courtroom linked arm-in-arm with a tall, red-haired woman who could have stepped from the fashion page of Vogue. Mark sensed I was upset and patted my hand. He was there for me. Had Paul ever truly there for me? I guessed she was the reason for this custody battle. She probably didn't want to ruin her waistline by having a kid of her own.

The day ended with little bloodshed drawn on either side. I think the lawyers were sizing each other up like two boxers in a ring. I left with Mark feeling hopeful, just the same. However, the second day turned out to be an entirely different story.

Paul gave the judge a terrible impression of me. He told the judge how my laziness and indifference drove him from our home. He recounted how I made him miserable by totally ignoring him after the baby was born. He had tears in his eyes when he told the court I had denied him his conjugal rights as a husband. I never even bothered to prepare any hot meals for him. I couldn't believe half of what I was hearing. Lies—it was all lies! I nearly jumped out of my chair to scream at him for lying, but Mr. Silver put his hand on my arm to restrain me.

Of course, I got to tell my side. After I was finished, Paul's lawyer tried to discredit me. He brought me to tears but didn't get me to say anything stupid or damaging. I couldn't wait to get out of that courtroom. What I experienced was worse than being stripped naked in public. I wanted to scratch out Paul's eyes and rip out his lying tongue for good measure.

Mark took me directly home after the trying time I'd had in court. Normally we'd discuss the outcome of the day at Mr. Silver's office, but I wasn't up to it. I just wanted to lie down and cry. Paul Jr. was taking a nap when we got back, so I went directly to my room.

His entire testimony replayed in my head over and over again. I couldn't get over the fact that I'd been once so in love with the man who could so easily fabricate such lies about me to the judge. Even on my worst days, I never neglected him or our baby. What hurt the worst was how he recounted the time when Paul Jr. was so ill, and he neglected to tell how he couldn't be bothered. Frightened and unsure of myself, I was left alone to care for a sick child. I found it hard to believe he could say such terrible things. He made me look like such a rotten person and a worse mother. I fell apart and cried.

Mark knocked on the door. "May I come in, Marisa?"

"Yes," I called out to him.

He came over to my bed and sat down. Putting his arm around me, he said, "Don't cry. No one in their sane minds will believe anything Paul or his lawyer said today." He wiggled his eyebrows and said, "Trust me. I'm sane and I don't believe any of it."

That made me chuckle. Somehow, he always got me to laugh with the crazy things he came out with.

"Good. That's better," he said as he gazed into my eyes. But the humorous moment was fleeting and soon replaced by tears as I buried my face in his chest. He kissed the top of my head and stroked my back until I finally stopped crying.

Mark put his hand gently under my chin and raised my head. Then he tenderly brushed my lips with his. It may have been a whisper of a kiss, but it sang through my veins. He sensed my reaction and kissed me again more passionately this time. Then in a flurry of hurried passionate kisses, he kissed my face and neck. I returned his kisses with a matching hunger. I needed him as much as I realized he wanted me.

Mark turned out to be a considerate lover. His lovemaking lacked the urgency of Paul's but turned out to be more satisfying. I'd fallen in love with my knight in shining armor.

That night after I put Paul Jr. to bed, I went to Mark's bedroom. The door was open, and I found him reading in bed. When he saw me, he broke into a smile and opened his arms. I glided into them as if I'd always belonged there. That day my marriage of convenience ended, and my real marriage was consummated.

We went back to court the next morning. I walked into the courtroom with a renewed spirit. Everything looked better that morning. Even Mr. Silver mentioned I was glowing and winked at Mark.

Paul's lawyer put his new wife on the stand. She testified how wonderful he was as a husband and provider. While she was being led through her testimony by the opposing lawyer, she slipped and said that she and Paul had begun seeing each other in October of the previous year. That would have been only two months after Paul Jr. was born and proved that Paul had been cheating on me.

Mr. Silver caught that right away. So did Paul because he covered his eyes with his hand. I wished I could be a fly on the wall of his bedroom that night. I wanted to thank the woman because it probably helped the judge decide in my favor. The most important fact, though, was that Paul Jr. wasn't ever going to be taken away from me.

As we walked out of court that day, I realized that my old life was finally over. I had begun a new beautiful one as Mrs. Mark Robertson. And I couldn't wait to spend my future with him.

THE END

NOW AND FOREVER
By Candace Gold

"Michael, get the phone, please! I'm full of suds."

"Sounds kinky," I said, entering the kitchen and saw my wife, Jamie, up to her elbows in soap, scrubbing a pot.

"Just answer the phone, funny boy."

"It's Sunnyhaven."

"Mom?"

I nodded.

Jamie wiped her hands on a dishtowel and grabbed the phone. I could see the fear and concern etched across her beautiful features. I reached for her free hand and held it tightly.

"Oh, no, no..." she said, collapsing into a chair. "Yes, I understand. I'll be there as soon as possible. Thank you."

Her tears were flowing full-force by the time she replaced the phone in its cradle.

"What's wrong?"

"Mom. She's in the hospital. They give her only a few days."

"I'm so sorry, sweetheart. But I thought she was in remission."

"The cancer worsened nearly over night. I should have been prepared—I knew this could happen..."

"No matter how long you know about it, you can never be ready. It always hurts," I

said enfolding her in my arms.

Jamie sobbed on my shoulder or a few moments. Then she grabbed a fresh tissue and blew her nose. A few minutes later, after she'd had her cry, she said, "I've got to call the airline and book the earliest flight out to Minnesota."

"I'll let Ed know when I see him tomorrow. I'm sure he'll understand."

"Thanks, dear," Jamie said as she began to dial the number of the airline.

Five minutes later, she said, "It's all set. I'll be taking the 10:53 flight. I'll drive the car to the airport and leave it there. Maybe you and Steve can pick it up later."

"Fine. Come to bed. You have a full day ahead of you."

When I took Jamie in my arms to kiss her goodnight, I had no idea how she would respond. It turned out she needed to be held and loved. It was as if she was trying to mask the pain, I knew she had to be feeling. Our lovemaking was slow and sweet, more of a comfort than a response to desire.

Jamie was my entire world. She was the secretary for Edward Chalmers, one of the partners at the law firm where I worked. You might say it was love at first sight. I saw her at the Christmas party and, like a magnet, was drawn to her. Blonde and blue-eyed as I am, she could have easily passed for my sister. But more than a physical resemblance, she turned out to be my soul mate. We began dating after that party and have been together ever since for the last five years. I've never regretted a moment. If something ever came between us, I wouldn't know what to do.

Jamie quickly fell asleep in my arms. Our lovemaking merely added to her mental exhaustion. She looked like a delicate angel as I watched her sleep. My heart ached with the love I felt for her.

***

In the morning, I kissed her goodbye and wished her a safe flight. She promised to

call when she got there and let me know what was going on. I had wanted to stay and have breakfast with her, but I was due in court early. It was a superficial civil case that I considered a nuisance one at best.

A couple was in the middle of a divorce where domestic fireworks had already been the norm, when the family dog, now living with the wife, bit the husband while he was retrieving some property from the house. He was suing on the grounds that the wife told the dog to bite him. I was representing the woman. As far as I was concerned, it was a case of spite and not worth litigation, but one of the partners thought otherwise. Today was the first day of jury selection.

***

When the court was dismissed for lunch, I crossed the street and headed towards my favorite luncheonette, a half-block away from the courthouse. It looked like a dive on the outside, but inside it had seats that were as comfortable as an old pair of jeans and served food that was downright delicious. As I walked, I thought about Jamie. She would be arriving in Duluth soon. I missed her terribly all ready and looked forward to her phone call.

Walking in, I noticed a small crowd standing around the television in the bar. Curiosity propelled me over. I walked over to Mark, the bartender.

"What's going on?"

"Another plane crash—"

"Where was it heading?" I asked.

"Minnesota, I think. It crashed right after takeoff. Engine trouble."

Suddenly my head began to throb as the blood in my veins turned to ice.

"Jamie... my wife... was taking a flight out this morning to Duluth," I said in a strange-sounding voice I hardly recognized as my own.

Before the bartender could reply, the reporter began to recap the news. I knew it had to be Jamie's flight even before the reporter mentioned it. How many flights to Duluth from Newark could there be? The tears stung my eyes. I began to bargain with God. Until I knew for sure Jamie was gone, I would literally cling to any possible hope. I surely would have traded my soul at this point until I heard the words I dreaded the most. "No known survivors..."

"No! Dear God, no!" I screamed out, as I felt my legs collapse from under me.

Moments later, Mark was pressing a glass in my hand. "Drink, Michael. It will help."

My tears were streaming down my face. I didn't care what the others might think. I had lost her. My life was over.

"Michael, are you one hundred percent certain your wife was on that flight?"

I nodded. "She's gone, Mark."

"So, sorry, man."

I didn't want his condolences or anyone else's. I wanted Jamie back.

The rest of the day became a blur. The crash was all over the news. I tried to get through to the airline. That was a joke. You'd think that with all the air disasters this country has experienced, they might have come up with a decent system of communication with the victims' loved ones by now. So, I spent the entire time practically glued to the TV. Not all the bodies were immediately located and there were still people who had been on the plane that were unaccounted for. Until they did, the authorities couldn't rule out the chance of survivors, though they didn't give the idea much merit. The plane had virtually been a fireball. By late afternoon the following day,

that slim door of hope had slammed shut.

***

It took another two days for the passenger list to be compiled. I had a few relatives who lived out of state to notify and had wanted to have the funeral as soon as possible so I could drink myself into oblivion. Then the airline authorities dropped a bomb into my lap. Jamie was not on the list of the dead.

How was that possible? Where else would she have been? I spoke to Tom Winters, the public relations person.

"How accurate is that passenger list that was printed?"

"Totally accurate, sir. Everybody was accounted for."

"Except my wife."

"Uh-huh. She was lucky. She wasn't on that plane."

"She had to be. She's not here."

"Maybe she changed her mind and flew to another destination. All I can tell you, Sir, is that Jamie Connelly was definitely not on flight 6783."

As I hung up with the man it hit me. I had totally forgotten that Jamie had driven to the airport. If there'd been some kind of mistake, her car would still be there. I called my friend, Steve, and asked him to drive with me to the airport to retrieve Jamie's car. I knew where to look for it because she told me she'd leave it as close to the flagpole as possible in the short-term parking lot.

Steve picked me up and we headed for the airport. I told him that Jamie wasn't on the plane.

"Wow! Did she take another plane?"

"I don't know. Where the Hell is she, Steve? She would have called me by now."

"You two didn't have a fight or something...I mean..."

"No. We were as close as ever. Jamie wasn't using her mother's illness as an excuse to run away."

"Sorry, bud, I had to ask."

"Maybe when we find the car we'll get some answers."

The car wasn't there. We searched the entire airport, but Jamie's Camry was nowhere to be found. I began to think that I was in the middle of some hideous nightmare that seemed to be worsening by the hour. Instead of getting answers, I was being bombarded by more questions.

"Steve, I want to believe that Jamie is alive. But why hasn't she come home or

gotten in touch with me?"

"Maybe she was in an auto accident and can't."

"But I would have been notified by the police. She had identification with her."

"Perhaps you should fill out a missing persons report."

"This is turning out to be one helluva nightmare."

I figured it was time to speak to the police. Steve would have driven me to the precinct, but he had a date a little later on.

"Just drop me off at the apartment. Thanks for your help, buddy."

"No sweat. Look, you're going to find Jamie."

"Yeah, sure..."

I knew I'd find her eventually. But would she be alive? I truly feared the worst at this point. There was a police car parked in front of my apartment. As Steve pulled to the curb, the two officers got out.

"Do you want me to come in with you?"

My stomach had already rolled over. I knew they hadn't come to tell me good news. I swallowed hard and said in a thin voice, "Nah. I can handle this. Go enjoy."

"You're sure?"

"Positive."

I got out and walked to my door. Steve waited, but I waved him away. The two officers approached me.

"Mr. Michael Connelly?"

I nodded. My heart dropped to my knees. Jamie was dead. I just knew it.

"May we come in?"

I nodded again and opened the door, fumbling somewhat with the key.

"My name is John Ryan and my partner is Peter Colby."

Both men shook my hand and sat down.

"This is the part of our job that we dislike the most," Colby said. "It's your wife. She was involved in an automobile accident with a chemical truck. Both vehicles went up in flames and both drivers were killed."

I began to laugh. They looked at me as if I were crazy.

"I'm sorry, but God must have a wicked sense of humor. You see, had Jamie not been killed in that car crash, she would have died on flight 6783. Either way, she would have been incinerated. Some joke, huh?"

"That's really rough. We're sorry, Mr. Connelly," Ryan said.

I nodded. By now my face was wet with tears. We talked for a few more minutes before they asked me to let them know where to send the remains. I told them that I would and let them out. By this time, the throbbing in my head had worsened and it felt as if it would explode.

I grabbed the first bottle I found and downed it. I didn't want to feel the pain anymore. In fact, I no longer cared to feel anything and wanted to die. Without Jamie, there wasn't much to live for, anyway. There would never be another woman like her. She had been made for me and now she was gone. End of story.

***

But I didn't die. Family and friends refused to allow me to exercise that choice. Instead they forced me to go on. They handed me the usual crap that Jamie wouldn't like me to give up, etc, etc. It was easier to agree than fight them. So I plunged into my work. Soon I was billing the most case hours in the history of the firm. I brought in a great deal of money and was soon offered a partnership. Not bad for a man who functioned like a robot. Time was supposed to heal all wounds. Well, let me tell you, it really doesn't. Only a thin scab would form and just the mere thought of Jamie would tear the wound wide open.

***

"Hey, Michael, are you free this Saturday?" Steve called to ask one night a year later.

"Nope. Too busy."

"Doing what? A monk has more action."

"I'm fine. Don't worry about me."

"You're not fine. Some of your body parts haven't been used in so long I'm

surprised they haven't shriveled up and fallen off."

"Not your concern, bud."

"Humor me. My girl has a friend. She's hot. What you say we all go out to dinner?"

"No thanks."

"It's only a dinner, for God's sake!"

"Leave him out of this. We're not on speaking terms."

"Will you go, just for me?"

I didn't want to waste my time or the girl's, but I did owe Steve, so I eventually agreed. Needless to say, the date turned out to be a disaster. I had nothing to say and ended up acting like one of the world's worst social misfits. On the bright side, at least Steve never asked me to double with him again.

Looking back on that dreadful night, I realized that I didn't set out to be a dud. My date was absolutely stunning, blonde and blue-eyed, with legs that never quit. It just happened. No woman could ever fill the place that had belonged to Jamie—not even temporarily. It didn't matter how much time passed, since time wasn't a factor. The simple truth was that there'd never be another woman I'd care to share my life with. Jamie had been one of a kind.

***

Three eternally long years have passed since Jamie's death. I had been made a partner in the law firm and now earn more money than I need. And making good investments has netted me more. I would often chuckle to myself thinking about all the wonderful things I could have given Jamie, but the tears always drowned out everything. What was the use? I was only sticking around this God-forsaken place until I could rejoin Jamie.

***

One afternoon I met Steve downtown for lunch. I could see that there was something on his mind. He could never make a convincing liar and was a worse poker player. I figured it was about one of his cases.

When the waitress came to take our orders and Steve asked for a Manhattan straight up, I knew he was really troubled about something.

"Want to talk about it, buddy?"

"Yes and no."

"Good answer. By any chance, are you a lawyer?"

"No, seriously, I've been kicking this around for a few days now. It's a no-win situation."

"It looks like it's getting to you."

"It is."

"Who's it about?"

"You."

"Me?"

"We been friends since law school and have been through a crap-load of things
together."

I smiled, thinking back. "That's for sure."

"I don't want you to go crazy about this—See, you're doing it already."

"What?"

"Getting upset."

"No! No, I'm not," I said, catching myself. "Please tell me. I have a right to know."

"I have a funny feeling that I'm going to regret this, but.... Did Jamie have a sister?"

"No, she was an only child. Why do you ask?"

"Just wondering."

"No, you weren't. What's going on?"

"Calm down. This is the very reason why I hate to bring up the subject of Jamie."

He was right. The very thought of Jamie still had the power to bring me to my knees. My heart ached terribly for her and always would.

"Okay, I'm calm," I lied. "Now tell me what the hell's going on."

"This is probably nothing. I saw a woman who resembled Jamie crossing the street in front of my car."

"Where?"

"By the post office. She was holding manila envelopes."

"How did she look?"

"I guess the same. Long blonde hair. Look, I could be wrong..."

"Maybe."

"Or maybe, it _was_ her.

"Look, I wasn't that close. Don't get your hopes up."

My mind was spinning with the news. Just think if Steve had seen Jamie...But how was that possible? Jamie was dead. She'd been killed in a fatal auto mishap...

"Michael?"

"Sorry. Anything else you can tell me about the woman?"

"Unfortunately, no. The light changed and I had to go."

Could it be possible? I realized what I was doing and it was crazy. Steve quickly

changed the subject. Perhaps he'd been reading my mind, as well. The conversation had to end though. Both of us had to head back to work.

***

Later that night as I lay in bed staring at the ceiling, I thought about what Steve had told me. Logically, it had to be a close resemblance and nothing more. Besides, didn't I hear that there was supposedly a double for all of us floating around somewhere out there? Despite that, I fell asleep, crying, with Jamie's name on my lips.

***

I had pushed the incident with Steve to the back of my mind and would have

probably left it there had my next door neighbor not approached me with the same

question. That, my friend, was too much coincidence for me. I had to see this woman for myself. I reasoned that she had to live or work in the area. That meant I had to run into her sometime. Unfortunately, I didn't have the patience to wait.

I tried hanging around the places where she'd already been seen, but had no luck. I began to think the whole thing was a fluke when no one else saw her, either. The woman might have been passing through or visiting.

***

Then on a Saturday morning, about two weeks later, I realized that if I didn't go to the supermarket, I'd have nothing in the apartment to eat. Not that food mattered much to me anymore. If I got hungry, I'd open a can of soup. Now I didn't even have as much as one can in the entire place. Throwing on a pair of old sweats, I drove to the supermarket. A word to the wise, don't ever shop on an empty stomach. You'll buy practically everything you see.

I was rounding the cookie aisle when I saw her. If it wasn't Jamie, it was her identical twin. My heart began to pound. I had to talk to her. I had to hear her voice.

As I neared her, I knew it had to be Jamie. There had to be an explanation. This woman had the same delicate nose and sensual mouth as Jamie. But her eyes...how many women had blue eyes that were as deep as indigo? At this point, I could hardly breathe.

"Jamie! My God! You're alive!"

Frightened, the woman backed away. "Go away before I scream."

"No. Please don't do that. I didn't mean to startle you. Jamie, it's Michael. Don't you recognize me? I'm your husband, for God's sake!"

"Look, I've never seen you before in my life."

This was truly a nightmare. The woman even sounded like Jamie, possessing a mid-western accent. It had to be Jamie. No other woman could look and sound exactly like her. It was impossible.

"But we're married—or we were, until you were supposedly killed in a car crash."

"You sound like you should be locked up or you have me mixed up with another

woman. Go away or I will scream!"

"I can explain—"

"You've explained enough," she said backing away.

I could see that she was about to freak, so I quickly pushed my cart into the next aisle. I was positive. However, there was absolutely no doubt in my mind. That woman was my Jamie. I couldn't merely let her slip away, though, now that I found her again.

She obviously didn't know me...There had to be an explanation...Suddenly it hit me. Amnesia. What if Jamie wasn't in the car? After all, she wasn't on the plane. Something traumatic could have happened to her that prevented her from being in the Camry. That would also account for her not remembering. I had to find out what happened to her that day, but how? The woman didn't even want to talk to me.

I quickly paid for the few things I needed and got into my car. I pulled closer to the exit and waited for Jamie to leave the store. At least I could find out where she lived by following her. Of course I needed to know what she was calling herself now, as well. Somehow I had to figure out a way to get her to trust me long enough so I could talk to her. However, that was going to be tough. She was obviously a frightened woman. The last thing I wanted to do was give her more grief.

As I waited for her to emerge from the store, my emotions were running amuck. Now that I knew she was alive, it was if I'd been reborn. No matter what, there was no way I'd ever rest until she was back in my arms.

She came out pushing a cart. I watched as she looked around a moment or two before she began to walk into the parking lot. Was all that apprehension caused by me? She approached a fairly new Camry and clicked open the trunk with a remote. As she put the groceries in the car, she cautiously looked all around once more. I began to think that her behavior was the result of something more ominous than me. After peering into the car and finding it safe to enter, she clicked open the car door and

scooted in.

I followed her out of the parking lot a healthy distance behind. I didn't want her to

spot me. From what I'd already seen, she'd probably freak out if she thought someone

was following her.

She drove to an apartment complex off of Main Street. I watched her park and slide her long shapely legs out of the car. Just seeing her do that caused a long forgotten stirring in my loins. After she unlocked the door to her apartment and brought her groceries inside, I left. Steve had a friend on the police force. Perhaps he who could run her license plate through the DMV and get me her name.

***

At first Steve was ready to send out to the funny farm for the men dressed in white when I told him that I was positive that the woman he saw was Jamie.

"You have no idea how much I regret telling you about this woman."

"But it _is_ Jamie. I should know. I lived with her."

"Michael, Jamie is dead."

"I spoke to the woman. She even had a slight accent."

"Coincidence. You're hearing and seeing what you want to. You <u>want</u> this woman to be Jamie."

"No, I'm not making anything up. She <u>really</u> is Jamie. Check out the license plate. There has to be an explanation."

"If it'll put this all to rest, I'll call Pete in the morning."

"You'll see. I'm not crazy."

"Yeah, sure. Just don't listen to yourself."

"I owe you for this."

"I can't believe that I'm aiding and abetting a crazy man. Perhaps I should get <u>my</u> head examined."

"Thanks, pal. You won't regret this."

"I already do."

"Hey look at it this way; if I don't find out her name, I really will go crazy."

He chuckled. "I'll make the call."

***

The next day I hardly put my cell phone down for a minute. I could barely keep my mind on my clients and their cases. I was never more certain that the woman was Jamie. All I needed was the confirmation. But, if she was using a different name, how would that help? I had to get more information about her.

I was a total stranger to her, which logically meant that she was suffering from some form of amnesia. I needed to understand more about it. This prompted me to call a psychiatrist whose services my law firm often used in order to get some answers. She agreed to meet me for lunch the following day. We decided on a restaurant close to both our offices. I hoped she could give me some useful information. Right now I felt as if I were grasping at straws.

***

Steve kept his word and had gotten in touch with his friend on the police force. When I arrived at the office the following day, he was waiting for me.

"I've got the woman's name. I think you'd better sit down."

In that second my heart skipped a beat.

"She's going by the name Jamie Buford."

"Th...that was Jamie's maiden name."

"I know."

"I don't care if you believe me or not. That woman is my Jamie. A coincidence won't cut it."

"I agree. If she honestly didn't recognize you may be right after all. She could be suffering from some form of amnesia."

"I intend to run it by Rosalind Decker when I have lunch with her later."

"I'm sorry I doubted you, Michael."

"How would you have known?"

"I hope you get her back," he said, turning to leave. "I'm due in court. Gotta go," he said, patting my shoulder.

"Thanks, Steve."

"See ya later."

After he left, I sat there a moment lost in thought. It was the first time in so long that I honestly felt hopeful. Perhaps there was a God up there after all and He finally decided to return from vacation.

***

Heads turned as the tall, attractive redhead walked towards my table. I had arrived for our lunch date a little early, hardly able to keep my mind on my work. I rose and pulled out her chair.

"You look lovely, as usual, Roz. Thanks for coming."

"Judging from the tone in your voice, you sounded anxious."

"Desperate is a more accurate description."

"Tell me about it. Perhaps I can help."

"You're aware that my wife, Jamie, was supposedly killed three years ago in a car crash."

"Why are you using the word 'supposedly'?"

"Because I have good reason to believe she is alive."

The waitress came over to take our orders and quickly disappeared, allowing me to continue. I told her about meeting the woman I believed to be Jamie and the fact she was using Jamie's maiden name. I told her everything I knew, which wasn't much, and asked if there was a credible medical explanation for all this, like amnesia.

"It would be easy to merely say yes to that, since it does sound like a form of amnesia. Without clinically speaking to this woman, it would be difficult to give you a definitive answer, which you're probably well aware of. Off the record, however, this is what I think:

"Since you're the one person who has been the closest to this woman, you'd be able to physically identify her. I'm comfortable with the knowledge that you think she's Jamie. If she didn't recognize you is using her former name, this tells me that the woman's reaching back to the apparent safety of an earlier time in her life before she experienced the trauma. The form of amnesia that she may have is a very selective one. She can remember everything up to a certain date. After that, nothing."

"Unfortunately, that period of time doesn't seem to include me in her life."

"No. However, with the help of a good therapist, there's always the chance she'll

eventually remember and invite you back into her life."

"Roz, to be perfectly honest. I can't wait that long. Every second she's away from me is torture."

"Then you are going to have to woo her all over again, keeping in mind that this time will be twice as hard. The trauma that caused the amnesia to begin with has undoubtedly scarred her."

"That would explain why she was so skittish."

"You're going to have to handle her with kid gloves. Anything you say, even body language, could spark a retreat if she's as apprehensive as you say."

"I know. I need to find out as much as possible about what happened to her, so I intend to hire Ross McAvoy."

"He's one of the best investigators out there, aggressive and thorough. If there's any info on Jamie to be found, he'll get it."

"Then, I'll have a better idea of what she experienced and how to deal with it."

"Having that knowledge and time are the best hopefuls you have. If she's under the care of a good therapist, maybe Ross McAvoy could get his or her name. Then perhaps you and the doctor can work together."

We talked a little longer before Roz had to return to her office to see a patient. I

sat and had a last cup of coffee, thinking about what she'd said.

When I returned to the office, Robin, my secretary, handed me a list of calls I'd gotten while I was out. Before I took care of them, I called Ross McAvoy. His secretary took my message and promised he'd return my call as soon as possible.

After speaking with Rosalind Decker, I knew that helping Jamie find her way back

was synonymous with rekindling our love. They were one in the same. In order to do so, I needed all the ammunition I could get from Ross. I hoped to hear from him soon.

I had returned most of the calls on Robin's list when she buzzed me that Ross was on the phone.

"Got a pretty skirt for me to chase?"

"This isn't for a court case, Ross."

"Personal, eh?"

"Very," I said, bringing Ross up to date on the roller coaster ride that my life had become.

"Okay. I'll do my best. You should hear from me within the week."

"Thanks, Ross."

"Is my usual retainer and other fees okay with you?"

"No problem. Money is no object."

"Good. Ciao."

The night before, I'd gone through Jamie's old telephone book that I'd found in her desk drawer. I wanted to find someone who knew the both of us. I was reaching, but I hoped that maybe if the three of us got together it could jar Jamie's memory. Carole Lombardi was the likely candidate, only the number listed was no longer in service. Information couldn't provide me with another. I hoped Ross McAvoy could locate her.

Jamie had known Carole a long time. They were such opposites, yet their differences probably brought them together. Carole had the more outgoing personality of the two, always laughing. We had gone out with Carole and her man of the hour a few times before she finally married and moved. I'm sure Jamie mentioned where Carole had gone, but I must confess that I paid little attention. And now, I was paying dearly for it. Had I known, I could have contacted Carole myself instead of having to wait for Ross to come up with the answers.

It all boiled down to time. I had all the time in the world when I thought that Jamie was gone, though it would have taken until eternity to finish grieving for her. Now that I knew she was alive, time became so crucial. Each minute Jamie remained out of my life was one minute less that I would be able to touch and love her. It was making me crazy.

***

Ross McAvoy called me five days later to set up a meeting. He had the info I'd requested and was certain it was complete as possible. We met at a small bar for a drink. From the moment I hung up the phone with Ross, until I saw him walking into the bar, I could think of nothing else.

He nodded and slid the envelope over to me. I took a smaller one out from my breast pocket and handed it to him.

"Thanks for compiling the information so quickly."

"Hey, man, if it were my wife, I'd want it done yesterday, as well."

Ross stayed for a drink and then left to see another client. I remained behind and read the report. It was complete and up to date. And, as far as I could tell, Ross left no stone unturned.

Two days after Jamie was supposed to have flown to Minnesota, she was found unconscious and near death by two teenagers in a wooded area along the Turnpike. She was nude and had been wrapped haphazardly in a torn tarp. Examination further revealed that she had been sexually assaulted. There was also a head wound caused by a blunt object. No identification had been left with the body. Gaining consciousness, days later, she told the authorities her name was Jamie Buford. The people living at the address she gave didn't know her. After being discharged from the hospital, she lived in a half-way house while undergoing both physical and mental therapy. She was still seeing a Myron Felton, a therapist affiliated with the hospital, once a week.

There was also a section on Carole Lombardi. It seems that after her failed

marriage, she returned to Jersey to live, and it turns out, we were practically neighbors. She had two boys, aged seven and ten, and a live-in boyfriend.

***

I called her that evening after I got home from work.

"Hello, is this Carole Lombardi?"

"It's Carole Browne again, but what's a divorce between friends—we are friends, I hope?"

She still had the same weird sense of humor that I remembered.

"I'd like to think we still are, Carole. This is Michael Connelly. You were a close friend of my wife, Jamie."

"Jamie! How is she? Come to think of it, why are you calling and not she?"

"Actually, she's the reason I'm calling. I have a problem and I'm positive that you're the only one who can help me with it."

"Listen, if it concerns Jamie, count me in. I miss her terribly."

"That makes two of us—"

"You two didn't split up, did ya?"

I told her the entire story with a few interruptions by what sounded like a herd of

wild children trying to kill one another. She apologized, though it was more comical than annoying. I knew she had a kind heart and had been close to Jamie, but she surprised me by wanting to help me plan everything. Without taking no as an answer, she invited me to dinner that same evening.

"Get your butt over here in fifteen minutes. We've got a great deal of planning to do."

"Yes, Commandant," I said, chuckling.

"And don't stop for wine, cake or anything else."

"I'm heading out now."

"Good."

I washed my face, ran a comb through my hair, and grabbed some photo albums. Grabbing my jacket and keys, I jumped into the car and drove to the apartment complex where Carole lived. She opened the door immediately.

"Hi, Carole."

"Come on in," she said hugging me. "You're a real sight for sore eyes."

I kissed her hello. She looked the same as I remembered her, a small, pixyish woman with short, jet-black hair and a perpetual smile. I knew she was sincere in her willingness to help. Jamie had once mentioned that she didn't think there was a mean bone in Carole's entire body.

She took my jacket and introduced me to a big guy dressed in a t-shirt and jeans. He had been wrestling with two boys and got up when I walked in.

"Michael, this is Ray."

He had a strong grip, but an easy smile.

"Glad to meet you, pal. I hope everything works out. If you need my help,

just holler."

"Thanks, Ray. I'll keep that in mind."

"Those wild Indians are Bobby and Brian," Carole said. "Wash up for dinner, boys!"

Dinner was an experience. The older boy, Brian, played hockey with his peas, while his brother made mashed potato sculptures on his plate. After dinner, knowing that Carole and I needed to talk, Ray occupied the boys. I had to hand it to him, the guy sure had stamina.

***

"Jamie and I lost contact a few months after I moved to New York. Charming Joe, who had transformed from a prince into a frog soon after I married him, was too possessive and extremely jealous of my friends. He kept me on a short, tight leash. Each year the leash got tighter and tighter, until I felt as if I was suffocating. Finally I cut the cord and moved back here. The only decent thing to come out of our union was the kids. After seeing them in action, I know it's probably hard to believe, but they kept me sane."

"They're nice, healthy boys."

"That's for sure. Did you two ever have kids?"

"We weren't able to."

"That's a shame. I know how much Jamie wanted kids. Maybe this time."

"I have to get her back into my life first."

"You will."

"I wish I had your confidence."

She gave me a huge, knowing kind of a smile before she said, "I have an idea that I think just might work. You'll meet Jamie here. I noticed you brought some photo albums. Good idea. I'll have Jamie over first without you. I'll tell her we have a mutual friend, show her the album pictures, and try to break the ice."

"What if she doesn't remember you?"

"She should if she seems to remember her earlier years like you say, but if she doesn't, I'll befriend her all over again. I'm sure she's been lonely."

"It shouldn't be too difficult for you to bump into Jamie. According to a private investigator I hired, she's a creature of habit. I'll write down some of the places she frequents and where she works."

"Michael, I'm a firm believer in 'love conquers all', despite everything. You've got to believe also."

I put my hand on hers and patted it. "Thanks."

"Don't thank me yet. Wait until next week."

By the time I left Carole's place, I was feeling the best I'd felt in a very long time. She would get the ball rolling and keep me apprised of what was happening. Okay, no matter how quickly things progressed, I was certain to become a basket case. After all, I had my entire future riding on this. The wonderful part was that at least now I had a future to look forward to. I just wished I had Carole's confidence.

***

A day later, Carole called with terrific news. Jamie had remembered her. She had met Jamie near her office and had invited her to dinner. When Jamie learned that Carole had two children, she couldn't wait to meet them. Unfortunately, I had to cut our conversation short because I was due in court. She promised to let me know how the dinner with Jamie turned out.

***

I had made an appointment to speak with Dr. Felton, the therapist who was treating Jamie since her mishap. He turned out to be a very conscientious man with a great deal of compassion. According to him, Jamie had made a great deal of progress over the last three years. He wasn't sure if she was capable of having a relationship yet but didn't rule it out. A wise man would leave the first move up to her. He thought that my coming back into her life could only be a positive thing and wished me luck.

***

Armed with Dr. Felton's hopeful words, I stopped by Carole's the night following her dinner with Jamie.

"It was weird. It was as if Jamie was stuck in time while the rest of us had moved

on. She made me feel so young again. But she honestly has no recollection of anything that's happened beyond our high school years."

"Did you show her the pictures?"

"Yes. I told her I got them from a friend."

"Did she ask you how this person got a hold of them?"

"Yes. I said that you were a distant cousin. After your disastrous first meeting, I was afraid to mention marriage."

"What you said was fine. I'll cross those turbulent waters after I've gained her friendship."

"She's coming to a party I'm giving Brian on Sunday afternoon."

"Great, I'll be there. Basically, what did she talk about?"

"High School."

I gave Carole a weak smile and shook my head.

"I know, Michael. She must have been through a terrible ordeal."

Tears welled in my eyes. "I love her so much that it tears me apart just to think about it."

"I promise to do whatever I can to help."

"I know. You've been wonderful so far," I said, hugging her. "I'm glad you're our friend."

When I let her go her eyes were wet also. I felt it was best to leave before we both broke down and bawled, so I said goodnight.

***

Sunday. Sunday was the day that could make or break my future. I actually made myself sick thinking about the possibilities. Knowing that I would soon be so close to Jamie, made me crazy, as well. All I could do now was pray that I said the right things and made all the right moves. If I scared her again, I'd probably never ever get another chance. Just thinking about what was at stake here tied my stomach into Gordian knots.

I arrived at Carole's early, my eyes glued on the door. When Jamie finally arrived carrying a gift, my heart leapt. She had swept her long, blonde hair up and held it with a clip. I had such a desire to take it down and run my hands through it as I often did when we were together. When she took her coat off, I could see she was wearing a simple, blue dress that couldn't hide her lovely figure and deepened the shade of her eyes, stirring still more memories and desire.

I was literally shaking the moment that Carole introduced us.

Jamie's eyes narrowed and I held my breath. "I know you...You're that strange

man from the supermarket!"

"I' m so sorry about that, but seeing you again after such a long, long time shook me up."

"Not as much as it did me. I thought you were crazy."

"I probably acted crazy. Please forgive me. I'm really very nice once you get to know me."

"I'll vouch for that," Carole added, placing her hand on my shoulder.

Carole's recommendation seemed to ease Jamie's suspicions about me. All during the party we talked. I had told her I was a cousin, related to Joe, her Aunt Evelyn's husband. She seemed to accept that. Things looked good until I asked her to have dinner with me. Her entire mien changed in an instant, making me fear that I may have rushed things.

"I'm sorry...I can't."

"Is it something that I said?"

"No. It's me."

"It's not like a date or anything...I mean we're relatives and all that. And there aren't too many of us left."

I watched her wring her hands as she gnawed her lip. She always chewed her bottom lip whenever she was deep in thought.

"I...I guess it will be okay..."

"It's only dinner—unless you want to catch a movie, too—"

"No! Just dinner will be fine."

Getting her to go out with me became the highlight of the day. Keeping my hands

off of her was the hardest thing I ever had to do, though. You have no idea how much I

longed to take her in my arms and kiss her.

***

The next day I sent her flowers. I knew that would put a smile on her beautiful face. I went into court that day and was brilliant. My roller coaster of a life seemed to be on the ascent, and I was going to ride it as far as I could. I would take one day at a time until I won her love back.

Perhaps Carole was right. Our getting back together again was meant to be. Why else would Jamie be alive? The ball was in my court and I was going to dribble it all the way to the basket. I had to be careful not to foul out, though.

***

The dinner date I had with Jamie was perfect. If I had rehearsed all my lines, I couldn't have done a better job. I knew enough of her life to talk about her relatives. The most important part was that she felt comfortable with me. That dinner date was followed by others. She began to trust me, little by little. I began to see glimpses of the person she once was. We were eventually able to go to the movies and concerts. I saw her at least three times a week. I knew she was enjoying my company and that was good. Keep in mind, though, during the entire time; I never gave her more than a chaste kiss goodnight on the cheek.

I remained in contact with Dr. Felton. He was now telling Jamie she'd been married, giving no specifics. That he left up to me. In turn, she told him about me and our friendship.

***

About four months later, Jamie invited me to her apartment for dinner. At that point, I truly knew she felt safe with me. I wasn't prepared for the conversation after dinner, though.

"I have something to ask you. I'm probably way out of line but...from the way you've acted towards me...I mean..."

I decided to put her out of her misery and make it a little easier for her to ask whatever she had on her mind. "What are you trying to ask? I'll be okay with whatever it is."

"You promise?"

I nodded and patted her hand.

"Are you gay?"

"What? Whatever gave you that idea?" I began to laugh."

"Well, you've never tried to touch me."

"Would you have liked me to?"

"I'm not sure. There were times when I think I'd like you to, but..."

"I didn't because I didn't want to hurt you in any way. Don't forget our first meeting."

Then for the first time, she opened up to me and mentioned that she was seeing a therapist.

"I felt confused, as if I were a puzzle with some pieces missing. Therapy has helped a great deal. The doctor explained to me about the gap I have in my memory. It's because something terrible happened to me."

"Do you remember what happened?"

"Only what the doctors told me."

"What did Dr. Felton say?"

"That I'd been attacked and left for dead. But they're only words and mean nothing to me."

"That's because your psyche is protecting you."

"You're the first person other than Dr. Felton who I can talk about this with. You've become my best friend, Michael."

"Would you like me to be more?"

She thought about my words a moment and smiled. "I think so. When I'm with you I feel so safe."

"That's a good sign."

"Why do you say that?"

"I must tell you something. I've been holding it in for a very long time."

"What?"

"Dr. Felton mentioned that you were married, right?"

"Yes, but I have no memory of it or the guy I was married to."

"Perhaps, you really do after all."

"Now you're confusing me."

"I'm your husband. I love you. I've always loved you, Jamie."

Before she could answer, I took her in my arms and kissed her. Whatever else I had to say she could tell from that kiss. I couldn't hold myself back any longer. To my surprise and relief, Jamie was actually kissing me back. How I had longed for this moment. Whether she remembered our love, or this was a new start didn't matter to me at this moment. Our kisses became more passionate, as my hands eagerly roamed the

body I loved until it was obvious there was no turning back.

I swept her up into my arms and carried her into the bedroom and laid her back

gently on the bed.

"Are you okay with this?" I asked.

She nodded and I kissed her with all the love I'd been storing all those empty years without her.

Making love to Jamie that night was akin to dying and going to heaven. I never made it home. Actually, home to me was wherever she was. We began a renewed relationship that night. I'd hoped that she would begin to remember bits of her past with me in it, but she didn't. Instead, I discovered that night was the beginning of an entirely new story for us. We had no past but were writing a bright future.

***

Nearly a year has passed. Jamie moved back into our old apartment. There are times when her mind seems to drift. However, when I ask her what she'd been thinking about, she doesn't have a clue. I know that eventually in time she will, but it doesn't matter to me. We'll deal with it. Right now, I'm the happiest man alive that I have her back.

Carole was right. Things did work out. But the scary part was that we just found out that Jamie was pregnant. How did she know about that as well? Either she was a witch, or the Lord did work in mysterious ways.

The End

TURNING BACK THE HANDS OF TIME
By
Candace Gold

As I washed the dinner dishes, I thought about how close Christmas was and having to celebrate it alone again this year, when the ringing of the telephone interrupted my thoughts. I shut the running water, wiped my hands on a towel, and picked up the phone before the answering machine did.

"Hello?"

"Rachel? Is this Rachel Taylor?"

"Yes. Who's this?"

"I'm so glad I reached you. It's Nancy Johnson from high school. Remember me? We had the same English class in our senior year. How are you?"

It took a moment or so for me to realize who was calling before a mental picture of Nancy flashed in my mind. I hadn't seen or spoken to her in nearly six years. Why would she be calling me *now?*

"I'm okay, Nancy. And you? It's been a *long* time."

"Yes, it has. I'm doing well. Look, I know you're probably surprised to hear from me..."

"That's for sure. How did you get my number, anyway?"

"I called every R. Taylor in the state, hoping to find you. It took a while, but at

last I found you."

"It's a great deal of trouble to go to just to say hello."

"Look, I'm calling from County General. I know it's really none of my business, but I felt you deserved to know."

"What?"

"Your father—"

"What about him?" I asked, feeling my throat close.

"He's in the hospital."

"Did he finally crash that old heap of his?"

"No. He's got stomach cancer."

"Oh, dear God! How bad?"

"It's the final stage. He's in a great deal of pain."

"Did he ask you to call me?"

"No. He doesn't know that I did."

"Then, *why* did you?"

"Because... because no matter what, I thought you'd want to be there with him."

"I appreciate your thoughtfulness, but..."

"Honestly, I wasn't certain that you'd be happy I called. It's just... I came on my shift one day and saw his name on the chart... Hey, if it were my dad, I'd want to know."

"But he's not. Look, thanks for letting me know—"

"You're not going to come to see him? He's dying, for God's sake—I'm sorry. It's really none of my business."

"You're right about that. Unfortunately, I doubt that he'll want to see me. After all, I wasn't the one who slammed the door between us."

"That was then. This is now. He knows he's dying. Maybe he wants to make

things right before he goes."

"And maybe he doesn't. He's a stubborn man."

"Look, I've got to start dispensing medication. If you do decide to come in, we'll have coffee together and talk."

"Nancy..."

"What?"

"Thanks for taking the time out to call. Despite my attitude, I appreciate it."

"I'm sure you would have done the same."

We said goodbye and I replaced the phone in its cradle. My hands were shaking. The news just sucked the air out of me. I thought my cantankerous old man would live forever. He's dying and still refused to break down and call. Maybe Nancy's wrong. Maybe he still wants to go to his grave angry. Even so, suddenly my life felt like a house of cards. The fragile world that had taken me years to construct was collapsing and disintegrating into rubble.

I still could recall every hurtful word he'd said to me the last time I saw him. And if I closed my eyes, I could still see his angry face as he spat, "If you leave this house now, Rachel, never come back." And as I slowly turned to walk away, he roughly grabbed my shoulders, spinning and me around to face him. "I mean it, child. You'll be dead to me just like her."

He was referring to my mother, of course, who had run off with some guy she met at a bar. In my father's eyes, I was running off and leaving him as she had done, even though there was no similarity between our actions. I was merely moving to an apartment in the city. It wasn't as if I was falling off the face of the earth and he'd never see me again. I'd call often and visit. But the scars of being left with a four-year-old child to raise on your own had never faded. He never got over my mother or what she'd done to him.

I let him cool down and waited a week or so before I called to say hello. I didn't want to leave things so poorly between us. After all, he was still my dad and I loved him, no matter how pig-headed he could be. Unfortunately, he hadn't cooled off one degree. The minute he heard my voice, he slammed down the receiver. I called back a number of times but got the same result. The loud click I heard each time severing the line reverberated in my ear long after I put the phone down. Eventually, I gave up trying to call and sent him cards and letters. They all were returned to me unopened. He wouldn't open the door when I went home for a visit, either. That was six long years ago.

Even if my father sees me, what will I say? How does one begin a conversation with someone you haven't spoken to in so long after the last words said between you were so harsh and unforgiving?

None of this would have happened had he tried to understand why I had to leave Carson. He refused to listen to a word I'd said, no matter how hard I tried to tell him. I just couldn't bear living there any longer, especially after— "Damn!" I slammed my hands down on the table and got up just as it all began to flow back, every memory, every thought, every feeling I tried to bury and forget. And I knew this time it wasn't going to stop.

I had to get this over with. I had to go see him. What if I didn't and he passed on? I'd end up adding more guilt to the mountain I'd been living with.

I brushed my hair. It was as black as my mood had become. I grabbed my jacket

and purse and jumped into my car. As I put the car in reverse, time seemed to roll back

as well...

*****

I saw Cord's smiling face. It was the day we first met at the state fair. My friend, Sandy and I had decided to go at the last minute. She had just gotten her license and borrowed her mom's car. Hungry, we were standing on line at one of the snack bars.

He came up behind us muttering to himself, trying to remember all the stuff he had to get. I turned around and he got this "I feel so stupid look" plastered all over his face.

"Gotta buy a lot of stuff. Almost a small army," he said attempting to explain.

"Big family?"

"Not really. Everyone just wants something different."

"I don't envy you. You live around here?"

"Yeah. We just moved here from Jacksonville. My name's Cord MacAllister."

"Rachel Taylor," I said shaking his hand and Nancy did the same.

"Will you be going to Taft High?" I asked.

"Uh-huh."

We talked until Sandy and I were waited on. After Cord delivered the food to his family, he came back and hung out with us. All I saw were those gorgeous blue eyes and dimples. I had fallen in love with him that very first night. We began to date, and I soon realized that he felt the same way about me. For the next two years, we were inseparable and were going to get engaged after we graduated.

I adored Cord and really thought he loved me too. Perhaps he did, until the terrible night during our senior years when my entire world fell apart...

Sandy and I had an awful fight. I can't even remember what it was about. All I can recall was that it was over something stupid. Somehow it was blown out of proportion and we ended up saying a lot of nasty things to one another. It had been the culmination of a bad week for both of us. Sandy had broken up with her boyfriend, Don, and Cord and I had a humdinger of a fight. But I never expected her to be so spiteful and do what she did. Looking back, I don't think that it worked out the way she'd planned it. I think things sort of spiraled out of hand and went too far. And, in the end, it all backfired. Even so, the ends justified the means, or whatever, and she ultimately destroyed our friendship and my life.

That weekend following our argument, Cord and I didn't see each other. Instead, he and a couple of other friends crashed at this guy's house whose parents were away. From what I heard, a lot of drinking was going on. Sandy crashed the party. She and Cord got it on. To make a very long and painful story for me short, she got pregnant and the two of them got married a few months later.

I wouldn't speak to Sandy, but Cord tried to explain himself to me. I couldn't bear to look at him, let alone listen. I felt betrayed and hurt by the two people I had cared for the most. Every time I saw them together or even heard anything about them, a little more of me died. After graduation, I applied for a job in the city and rented a room in a boarding house. I desperately tried to explain to my father why I needed to go, but he wouldn't listen.

I never spoke to Cord or Sandy again. Somehow, I found out that they had a little girl. I think she was named Belinda.

By the time I pulled into the parking lot at the hospital, I needed a new pack of tissues. Why can't some wounds ever heal?

I walked into the hospital and inquired about my father. He was on the third floor.

I never liked hospitals with their own smells and washed-out green walls. It was like entering another world, one preoccupied with sickness, and too often, death. As I got into the elevator, I knew this was probably the last time I'd ever see him. I had to talk to him, no matter what. I needed to tell him that I still loved him despite everything. I wasn't my mother. Hell, I didn't even know her.

Nancy was at the desk facing the elevator when it opened. She got up and greeted me. "I'm glad you decided to come," she said and hugged me. "You look the same."

So, did she. Chubby, always smiling, and there to help anyone who needed it. Was it any wonder she became a nurse?

"I just checked on him. He's awake. I wish I could tell you that he was resting comfortably, but I can't."

"Thanks. Now if he only talks to me…"

"Good luck."

"I think a small miracle would be in order now."

Nancy smiled and gave me a push. "Go. You won't know until you try."

I slowly walked towards room 335. As much as I wanted to do this, I found it difficult. I almost wished that he'd be asleep. I guess I was being somewhat of a coward, not wanting to have my head bitten off.

The door was open. It was unearthly quiet in the room as I walked towards the bed. The black man lying there hardly resembled the man I'd left six years ago. He looked old and shrunken beyond his years, a shell of the man he once was. Tears began to well in my eyes. Sensing that someone had entered the room, he opened his eyes.

"Dad?" I whispered, softly.

He squeezed his eyes tightly closed perhaps to make me disappear. "Go away."

"Dad, please. I want— no, I must talk to you. There's so much to say. Please look at me."

There was no response. Perhaps he was too weak to make a scene. Maybe part of what I'd say would reach his ears or breach the wall in his heart.

"What's past is past. I'm here for you now, Dad. It's been a long time and I've missed you so. I've never stopped loving you, you know. I have a good job now and just got a promotion..."

I realized that I was just rambling on, but there was so much that needed to be said. My father remained silent, so I had no indication if he was even listening to me. When Nancy came walking in with some medication for him, she gave me a questioning look as if to ask how things were going. All I could do was shrug, for I had no idea myself.

"Mr. Taylor, it's time for your medication," she said, pouring fresh water into his cup.

My father's hand shook as he took the water and the pills from Nancy.

"I'll help him, Nancy," I said, helping him steady the cup. Surprisingly, he didn't pull away. I took that as a positive thing. Looking into his eyes, I noticed some tears. I wondered if they were because of me being there or the pain from the cancer.

Nancy smiled at me and left.

"Dad, I know you never realized this because you were too angry and hurt at the time, but you closed me out of your life very much the same way Mom hurt us. You orphaned me that day. I felt so low that I wanted to die."

Even though my father said nothing, a tear slid out of his eye and down his face. He quickly wiped it with his hand, probably hoping that I wouldn't notice. I decided that maybe I should leave and come back tomorrow. Maybe the shock of seeing me would be over. I was about to tell him I was going when he began to speak.

"I'm dying, Rachel. I'm not walking out of here."

"Of course, you will," I said, not truly believing it.

He shook his head. "Come sit closer. I don't have the strength to talk too loudly."

I welcomed his feistiness and found it reassuring. Suddenly his face contorted and darkened as he clutched his middle.

"Are you in pain? Shall I call, Nancy?" I said, already out of my chair.

"No," he said barely over a whisper.

"Water?"

He nodded and I helped him drink some. When he was able to speak once more, he said, "This damned cancer is God's punishment for abandoning you."

"No, Dad. God doesn't do that."

"I was a stubborn, prideful man. You were a good girl."

"And I have you to thank for that. You shaped the person I am today single-handedly."

"And I threw it all away."

"No, you didn't. I'm here now and I won't leave you again."

He raised his hand and I took it. I brought it to my mouth and kissed it. Then I lay my head down next to his. I had dreamed of seeing him again so many times over the past six years. I just never expected it would be like this.

"Oh, Dad, I love you so. We're going to beat this thing together."

He seemed too exhausted to argue.

"Maybe you should try and get some sleep. I'll be back tomorrow."

I kissed him goodnight and walked out, a mixed bundle of emotions. Nancy was at the desk. I walked over to her.

"How'd it go, Rachel?"

"Better than I ever imagined."

"The good part is that you two are speaking together again."

"He thinks God gave him cancer as punishment."

"Many of the older people think like that. I hear it all the time."

"So, it's the guilt brought on by the cancer that knocked some sense into my Dad."

"Does it matter what brought him back to you?"

"I guess not," I said shaking my head. This gives new meaning to God works in mysterious ways."

"And what about you? How are you feeling?"

"Shocked, drained, but happy to get Dad back—but not thrilled with the fact it won't be for long."

"So, make it last as long as you can. Give him the love you saved all these years."

"I'll try," I said.

"It won't be easy watching him die a little with each passing day."

"I know. I'm just as scared as he is. I hardly recognized him."

"Life is so short. Keeping this in mind, why do we act the way we do?" she asked.

"Good question."

"Well, the good part is that you've been reunited. That's got to be a relief for you."

"That's for sure. The last six years I felt so alone—especially on the holidays."

"Look, I'm getting off soon. Would you like to go for coffee and talk?"

"I think I need something stronger," I admitted.

"How about stopping at Ryan's then?"

"That's fine, thanks. I can use someone to talk to."

I went to the lounge to wait for Nancy's shift to end. She was such a sweet person. It was strange that we never became friends in high school. I guess we didn't hang out with the same people. Nancy and I were cheerleaders and outgoing, while she was quieter and more bookish. In all my visual memories of her, I always saw her reading a book.

Sitting and sipping coffee, I gazed up at the TV. Some old movie was on, but in my mind, I changed the faces of the actors. I saw Cord and myself on one of the many happy occasions. I could almost feel the touch of his lips on mine. Then Nancy appeared and ruined everything, just as she had a thousand times in my memory. I was so absorbed with the past; I hadn't heard Nancy enter the room.

"Ready to go?" she asked, breaking the spell.

"Yes, most definitely."

I followed Nancy to Ryan's a local bar not too far from where I'd once lived. It was still hopping. I could hardly remember the last time I'd been there. Cord and I used to stop in for a drink with friends. When I left Carson, I never returned to any of the places we used to go as a couple. I feared running into him and Nancy.

It was noisy enough that you could talk, and no one could overhear what you were saying. We found two empty seats at the end of the bar opposite the jukebox and ordered two beers.

"I'm truly glad you called me, Nancy. I can't thank you enough."

"I'm glad I did also. In a small town like this, everyone knows each other's business. I knew what happened between you and your Dad. If it had been mine, I doubt if I could have handled it as well."

"Life goes on. You take one day at a time. I couldn't do what you do every day."

She sighed. "Sometimes I wonder how I do it myself. You see so much..."

"I just can't believe what the cancer has done to him. He was such a strong man."

"I know."

"I can't help thinking I wouldn't be sitting here had you not called."

"Don't make me a saint. It was only a phone call."

"No matter how you try to minimize it, Nancy, I'll always be grateful. I..."

A song began to play on the jukebox. My heart nearly skipped a beat. It was our

song—Cord's and mine. The one we both loved and would have danced to at our wedding.

"Rachel, are you okay?"

A moment passed before I could breathe, let alone speak. I nodded and turned towards the jukebox. My body turned to jelly, and I nearly slid off the chair when I saw him standing there, arms braced against the machine. He must have sensed someone watching him because he slowly turned around. Our eyes met.

I threw down some money to cover my drink. "Gotta run, Nancy," I said, fleeing from the bar on rubbery legs.

I ran to my car, half-stumbling through the gravel. Fumbling in my purse for my keys, I tried to steady my shaking hands. I could hardly see through my veil of tears. I found the key and wrestled it into the lock. I slid into the car and was about to close the door when I felt resistance.

"Rachel! Don't go!"

Cord had followed me out of the bar. I pulled on the door. "Let me be!" I pleaded, nearly choking on my tears. I didn't want him to see me cry.

"Why won't you talk to me?"

"We have nothing to say. Go home to your wife and kid," I spat, grabbing the door and finally closing it.

I started the engine and tore out of the lot like some crazed person. Looking back in the mirror, I saw him standing there. I only got as far as two blocks before a cascade of tears blinded me, forcing me to pull to the side of the road. Discovering that I still cared for Cord hurt almost as much as seeing him again. I had made a vow long ago never to let him know.

I remained at the side of the road until I had regained control over my emotions. Heading back into the city, I rehashed the roller coaster ride of a night I'd had and made plans to be able to spend time with my father. When I finally fell into bed and closed my eyes, Cord's face appeared before me. Would I ever be free of him?

I called my personnel director the next day and requested a leave of absence. He was very understanding and told me to take as much time as I needed. Working for a large corporation does have its perks. Then I packed some clothes and took a room at the closest motel to the hospital. I didn't want to have to drive two hours back and forth each day.

When I got to the hospital, I went to speak to Dr. Reisman, my father's oncologist. I wanted to know exactly how bad the cancer was and how much time was left. As much as it hurt, I was trying to be a realist.

Dr. Reisman was young. I had expected a much older person. He was slightly built with thin brown hair. I was drawn to his large, brown sympathetic eyes.

"I won't lie to you, Rachel. It's bad. The cancer has already spread to surrounding organs."

"Isn't there anything you can do?" I asked, trying to keep my throat from closing.

"At this point, all that can be done is to make him as comfortable as possible."

"Then, there's not much time left, is there?"

"I'm afraid not. "Weeks... a month at best."

"Oh, dear God," I said, suddenly feeling sick as my knees nearly buckled.

"Are you all right?" the doctor asked, reaching for me in case I fell.

"Yes. Just give me a moment to catch my breath."

Dr. Reisman poured me some water. I sipped it slowly.

"Does he know?" I finally asked.

"I imagine he surmises. He's in a great deal of pain. I doubt that he believes he's going to recover at this point."

I swiped away my tears. There would be very little time left to cram in everything that I would like to. I'm certain he's already regretting the time lost. I'd make sure what was left would be quality time. "I'll be with him."

"I'm glad that he'll have a loved one by his side."

"Thank you, Dr. Reisman."

He patted my hand. I imagined he did that a great deal. How was he able to sleep at night and not be haunted by his patients? How much of him was chipped away with every lost soul? I left his office and stepped into the bathroom to wash my face before I went to see my father.

My Father's eyes were closed when I walked into the room. I went to sit down quietly in the corner.

"Come closer so I can see you," he said, nearly unnerving me.

"I thought you were asleep."

"Just resting my eyes."

"How're you feeling today?"

"Not fit to go dancing. You speak to the doc yet?"

"Uh-huh."

"What did he tell you? I can't pin that medicine man down and get a damn answer worth spit."

"He says the cancer is bad."

"You think I don't know that? How much time did he say I had?"

"Not much."

"How much is not much?"

"Weeks, a month," I said nearly choking on the words.

He nodded. "He asked me if I wanted to go to a hospice."

"And do you?"

"Nah. They treat me good here. Besides, if I have so little time left, why bother?"

"You can always change your mind."

"I won't. You married yet?"

"No, Dad."

"Too bad. I wanted to bounce some gran kids on my knee."

"I've got a good job, though."

"You happy?"

"I guess."

"You're not sure?"

"Pretty sure," I answered wanting to get off the topic.

"Tell me about your job," he managed to say before he winced.

"Are you in pain? Should I call the nurse?"

"Girl, it's constant. Sometimes it just worsens. It'll pass."

We talked until he was given some medicine and fell asleep. I took that time to stretch my legs and get a bite to eat. He waked a short time after I had returned to his room. We talked some more before he grew tired and fell asleep again. Basically, he dozed on and off all day. I tried to be there whenever he was up and alert.

Nancy came in to say hello when she came on duty. Later on, when she took her break, she asked me to have a cup of coffee with her. I sensed that she had something important to tell me.

"I'm going to get right to the point, Rachel."

"This sounds serious."

"Last night after you left the bar, Cord poured out his heart to me—"

"Stop right there," I said holding up my hand and rising from my chair. "I'm not interested in anything that concerns Cord."

"He said you'd react this way. What harm is there to hear what he told me?"

I shook my head and raised my hands as if to ward off her words.

"Why are you still running away?"

I didn't answer. She continued. "There's only one reason that I can think of. You're still in love with him, aren't you?"

I said nothing as I collapsed into the chair.

"You know, he still loves you too. Always has."

"He certainly had a funny way of showing it."

"It was a stupid mistake. He's still paying dearly for it."

"Yeah? Too bad."

"He was forced to marry Sandy. Her brother and two of his friends beat him up and put him in the hospital. And when he got out, he married her with a shotgun aimed at his back."

I never knew about that. Sandy's brother had been a wild one, running with the wrong crowd. But that still didn't excuse the fact that Cord got Sandy pregnant. "Well you play, you pay."

"He's never stopped paying. Ironically, it was Sandy's fault that it happened in the first place."

"Doesn't the guy always blame the girl?"

"Come on, Rachel, give it up. Cord had gone to Dan Reilly's house that night to get drunk. He had wanted to lick his wounds. You two had had a fight."

I found myself subconsciously nodding.

"Sandy showed up and threw herself at him."

"Probably to get even with me. We'd had a fight, as well."

"Cord said he was so drunk that he has no idea what when on between them. He only knows that he woke up in the same bed with her the following morning but has no recollection of having sex with her. He often wonders if the baby's father could have been one of the other guys."

"Is he still with Sandy?"

"No. They're divorced and in the middle of a custody battle over their daughter, Belinda."

"Why?" I asked. "Especially if the child might not be his."

"Sandy is an alcoholic. She can hardly take care of herself, let alone a child."

"Where's Belinda now?"

"Nancy's mother's got her. Cord loves the little girl, but they don't let him see her much."

"What a mess that turned out to be."

"Why don't you talk to Cord?" Nancy asked.

"I can't."

"All you're doing is pouring salt into the wound."

"Look, I really don't want to talk about this anymore. I've already heard more than I'd care to."

"Are you afraid that Cord will find out you still love him?"

I stopped dead in my tracks.

"God forbid you two kiss and makeup."

I turned around and shook my head. "There's too much hurt to get over. I don't want to go through all that again."

"And what are you doing now? Tell me you're not hurting."

"It's only because I saw him last night."

"That's a load of horse manure and you know it," Nancy said bluntly.

"Look, thanks for the advice, but I've gotta go. My father must be awake by now."

She placed her hand on my arm. "Rachel, when will you stop running from the truth?"

I didn't reply. Instead, I did what I do best—fled.

As I approached my father's room, I heard voices. I nearly died when I walked in and saw Cord sitting by his bed.

"Rachel, look who came to visit with me?" my father said, smiling widely.

"I see," I replied through clenched teeth. I knew how much my father had liked

Cord and didn't want to spoil the visit. That didn't stop me from falling apart inside. I

wasn't certain if I was more upset or angrier. It wasn't long before my dad fell asleep.

Cord and I walked outside.

"How dare you?" I spat.

"You know how much I liked your dad. Nancy told me how sick he was last night."

I had no comeback for that. "She told me you two talked."

"And?"

"What? I still have nothing to say to you," I said biting my lower lip to stop it from quivering. "You had your visit—go home."

"Can't we talk?"

"What for?"

Suddenly, Cord grabbed my shoulders, so I had to face him. "If nothing more than because you once loved me."

"No. It's a waste of time," I said trying to get away from him, but he held on tightly.

"I can't let you run away again. Not this time."

"Let me go, Cord." I struggled to be free of his grip.

"No. I've waited much too long to tell you what needs to be said. I never wanted to hurt you. Damn it, Rachel! I never stopped loving you," he said, crushing my mouth with his.

I wanted to fight him, push him away—anything. But I found myself returning the kiss with the same intensity. Tears seeped from my eyes and silently slid down my face as my lips clung to his. When we parted and I saw tears in his eyes.

"I love you!" he cried, as he sought my mouth again.

This time I felt his tears mingle with mine. I was lost. There was no way I could

run away from him, not then—not ever again.

"Cord."

Hearing my father's voice, we reluctantly separated and walked back inside his room. When Cord approached the bed, my dad reached for Cord's hand and pulled him close enough to whisper something in his ear. I wanted to find out what he'd said, but Nancy came by with some meds and it slipped my mind. She broke into a grin when she saw Cord and me together.

When Dad fell asleep, Cord and I left. We stopped to speak to Nancy. I walked over and we hugged one another. In her ear, I whispered, "Thank you from the bottom of my heart." She whispered back, "Just invite me to the wedding." Then she winked at Cord and he gave her a huge smile.

Cord and I went to a small diner down the road for something to eat. Actually, the only hunger we both seemed to have was for each other. We held hands the entire time. Perhaps he meant what he said about not letting me go literally.

We were having coffee when I remembered to ask Cord about what my dad had whispered to him.

"Oh, that. He told me to marry you as soon as possible. He said that no matter what you may say or do, you love me very much."

Tears began to fill my eyes. "He actually said that?"

"Yup," he said, stroking the side of my face with his hand. "And Daddy knows best, right?"

I took his hand and kissed it. "Uh-huh."

"Will you marry me, Rachel? Marry me tomorrow. For your dad."

I looked into those unforgettable beautiful eyes that haunted my soul for the last

six years and nodded. All I kept thinking was how did I exist all that time without him? And this Christmas would be the happiest I've had in a very long time. Marrying Cord and being together for the rest of our lives would be the ultimate Christmas gift to one another.

We had the wedding ceremony in my father's room. Nancy, and Cord's mom looked on as the minister pronounced as man and wife. My dad, despite the pain, appeared happy.

***

Dr. Reisman was right. My father passed away within the month. I took his death hard, but I had Cord and Nancy to lean on for support. During that time, Nancy and I became good friends.

I met Belinda, Cord's beautiful five-year-old daughter. The most noticeable thing about her was her beautiful gray eyes. Both Nancy and Cord had blue eyes. Perhaps she wasn't Cord's child after all, though it didn't seem to matter to him. Seeing how he was with her melted my heart.

Christmas night as Cord and I snuggled by the fire, he told me the rest of what my father had whispered to him that day. I guess it was a recipe for life. "Have many babies now and love them with all your heart and soul because before you know it, it's all gone."

I snuggled closer to Cord. "That's the best advice my dad ever gave. I reckon we should follow it."

"I reckon so," he said covering my mouth with his.

The End

Walk on By
By Candace Gold

It was raining again. I guess it began raining a great deal since Ron died, both literary and figuratively. Perhaps a cloud rolled in over Long Island the day he lost his battle with lung cancer. I've been told it's all part of the grieving process and things will get better. Time heals everything. Really? And in how many more years? 10? 20? 50? I sighed, doubting the hurt from his loss would ever be healed. Perhaps lessened with time, but never completely gone.

When I walk through this house, I can't help but see him in every room. This was our first home together where we had our children watched them grow. Sammy, our redheaded little boy, and Renée, the blonde sweetheart who followed her older brother everywhere he went. Now they are both grown with children of their own. And this house is so empty.

The memories that are part of this house pull at me from all directions. Honestly, I doubt they will ever let me go as long as I remain here. It just might be time for me to leave them and the house behind. I truly needed to get on with my life. Ron would probably be the first to tell me so. And that left me with a major decision. Where would I go?

Realizing I had several choices, I firmly wrote off two. I would never live with either of my children. Renée already offered at least a half dozen times for me to move in with her, but she has her own family to care for and doesn't need an extra worry. Though I was an active 70-year-old, I knew the rest of the way would be downhill. Things happen, life happens, it just was that way.

No, I wouldn't be a burden to either child and would live in my own place until the time came when I couldn't fend for myself. Then I'd probably be shuffled off to some old age home. What if I combined the two?

A friend of mine who now lived in Florida moved into an assisted living complex with her husband. There were doctors and nurses on staff to help if either of them needed it. When they became incapacitated, they were able to move into an apartment in the nursing facility which was part of the complex. They could give up their independence at any time. This sounded very sensible to me. The bottom line here was that they were happy with the arrangement. These assisted-living complexes were cropping up all over the country, but I wanted to remain near my daughter. The main reason was that Maine, where Sammy and his family lived, was too cold and I had no desire to move there. His children were older than Renée's and could travel better. Still, I didn't take this decision lightly and had a lot of research to do.

Ironically, both my kids kept hinting and then became more obvious as time went by, that I had to downsize and move out of the house. Up until this point, I was not in favor of doing so. Now that the time is right, I can just imagine their faces telling them of my decision.

On Sunday I sat down with the newspaper and poured through the real estate section with its ads for apartments and condos. Along with those were pages of nursing homes and several established assisted-living complexes already operating on Long Island where I now lived. Then the full-page ad for the grand opening of a new complex caught my eye. It wasn't located too far from my daughter's home. With nothing to lose and everything to gain, I decided to drive over and check the place out.

I was quite surprised by the enormity of the place. It was divided into sections. In the high rise was the living areas where they offered studio apartments up to three-bedroom apartments for those people who like to have visitors. The dining room was situated on the first floor. Then there was the recreation area where they had club meetings, a gym, and pool, auditorium for dances and movies, a beauty salon, sauna, hot tub, and spa. Then there was the nursing home and hospital.

For me, one or two bedrooms were just fine, so I had a lovely woman who was giving me a tour of the place show me those particular apartments.

Not to bore you with the mundane tour and my putting a binder on a lovely one-bedroom apartment, let's just say I was more than impressed with the facility. I truly liked the fact that I wouldn't need to go elsewhere to have my hair or nails done or see a movie. If I got sick the doctors and nurses on the premises would take care of me. And if I ever required a hospital, there was one located on the other side of the complex. When the time came that I could not live alone any longer, there would be a place for me in another part of the complex. There I could have 24/7 care.

I was certain my children would approve of my decision and couldn't wait to tell them. I knew everyone would be together at Thanksgiving, which was usually held in my house, but there was so much to do, and I knew I couldn't do it alone without their help. So, I had to spill the beans.

We had a conference call and I told them of my plans. My daughter's friend listed my home. Then Renée and my son-in-law, Peter, came on the following weekend to help me pack some things away. This scenario was repeated several times until whatever I was taking with me was packed and those things that needed to be removed were gone. Whatever furniture Renée could use was placed in a U-Haul and driven to their house. I ended up giving the rest to Goodwill.

By the time I intended to move into my new place, the house had sold. Luckily a young couple was looking for a place on the North Shore and my house appeared to be the right one for them. They gave me my asking price, wanting to move in as quickly as possible. Renée and Peter helped me finish packing up the house. Pots, Pans, glasses, and silverware needed to be boxed so they could be transported to my new apartment. Linens and towels and cleaning stuff had to go as well. In two days, I would be able to start moving into my apartment. I felt like I once did with Ron when we moved into our own place.

I was able to bring some stuff over, but on the weekend, Sammy flew down from Maine and joined Renée, Peter and me to help finish stocking my apartment. It was beginning to look like a home. As soon as my bedroom set arrived, I'd officially move in. Actually, I couldn't wait to get out of the motel I was staying in. I was giving the kids a tour of the entire facility and heading to the building where the dining room was located when I heard my name being called.

"Marlene? Marlene Jacobson?"

We all turned to face a man around my age with solid white hair and a beautiful smile. Jacobson had been my maiden name, so he had to have known me before I had gotten married to Ron and changed my name to Greene. Slowly, the realization who he was came to me like a lightning bolt piercing my heart. His name, Richard Flynn reverberated in my head like an echo that couldn't stop repeating itself.

Rich had been my first love. He was the guy I was supposed to share my life with. Though he'd changed dramatically as I had, those adorable dimples and twinkling blue eyes were still evident. He'd aged handsomely, still possessing a full head of hair. The hair I used to thread my fingers through. It was that thick.

He spoke and pulled me from my reverie. "I wasn't certain it was you until I heard you speak. Then I knew," he said as he approached us. "Hello, Marlene. It's been way too long," he said as he tried to embrace me. My reaction probably stunned everyone. I moved quickly to evade his touch.

"It certainly has," I replied, trying not to say how glad I was about that. The next moment brought on the rest of the memory, hard and fast, as the hurt nearly brought me to my knees. "We've got to run," was all I said and rushed off with my two kids trying to catch up with me.

"Mom, wait," Sammy called and then looked back to see the man still standing there watching.

"What's wrong, Mom?" Renée asked as soon as we were outside.

"I don't want to live here anymore. I'm going to cancel my lease."

"What?" both kids said in unison. They looked at me as if I'd just lost my mind.

Perhaps I did sound a little crazy. I'd been so in love with Rich and I truly thought he'd felt the same way about me. How could I explain the hurt I felt just bumping into him after all these years? And what if I saw him all the time? Obviously, seeing me again didn't bother Rich Flynn, however, he wasn't the one whose life was turned inside out.

My kids steered me to an empty bench under a glorious oak tree. I needed to sit. The shock of seeing Rich had sapped my strength.

"Okay, we need to talk about this," Renée said.

"That's for sure," Sammy chimed in.

"There's nothing to talk about," I said quietly.

"I think there is, Mom, big time. One minute you're loving this place and then you're not. That guy, whoever is he, is the major factor in changing your mind," Sammy said.

"Whatever happened to our levelheaded mother?" Renée added.

"Who was the man and what happened between the two of you?" Sammy probed further.

When I remained reticent, Renée said, "You do realize that if you cancel your lease you will have no place to live. You will have to store all your things in a storage facility and probably lose a bundle of cash in the process. Think about the practical side of things."

"In other words, don't make any rash decisions," Sammy said.

"So, let's discuss this now while we're all together," Renée said, reminding me that Sammy had to fly home later that night.

"You're not going to drop this, are you?" I asked my children.

"Absolutely not," Sammy replied. "How can I fly home knowing your future is in doubt?"

"Aren't you make a mountain out of a molehill," I said, instantly regretting it.

"Who's creating mountains?" Sammy challenged.

"So, what went on between you both?" my daughter asked.

I sighed, knowing I had to tell them. They just didn't seem to be a way around it.

"Mom..." Renée prompted.

"Way back in high school, that guy, Rich Flynn, had been my steady boyfriend for over three years. He had been my first real love."

"So, what happened, Ma?" Sammy asked.

"To tell you the truth, I'm not too sure what really happened between us. One day we were together and the next we weren't."

"Something had to happen to break you two apart," Renée said.

"I think his father played a big part in breaking us up. Mr. Flynn was the CEO of some big corporation. The name escapes me right now. He wanted his son to follow in his footsteps by marrying a rich woman as he had. As for your grandfather, he was a peon compared to a wealthy CEO. Therefore, his daughter was deemed unworthy."

"I thought that stuff went by the way of the wayside and people married for love," Renée said.

"On that, we agree. Only my story with Rich just didn't have a happy ending. I thought he loved me too— or enough to combat the will of his father. Unfortunately, he wasn't that strong and ended up marrying someone his father had picked. All I know about her was that she was very, very rich.

"Rich told me two days before the prom that he couldn't take me. He didn't even have the nerve to tell me to my face. Instead, he called me on the phone. And that was the last time I spoke to him."

"Boy, he's some piece of work," Sammy said. "I can understand how you feel about him, but—"

"Are you going to let him hurt you again by not moving in here?" Renée interrupted. She looked like she was ready to go back and slug the guy.

"You don't have to see or talk to him if you don't want to," Sammy said.

"Easier said than done," I answered.

"Not really. Ignore him. That would bug any person," Renée added.

"You said he got married, right, Mom?" Sammy said.

"Yes."

"And yet, he was alone. There was no one with him," Sammy continued.

"There could be a dozen reasons for that. Besides, what difference does it make?" I asked.

"And, how do we know that he actually lives there?" Sammy asked.

"Yeah. He could be visiting a friend or relative," Renée added.

"Look, all this doesn't matter one iota. It's your happiness that matters, Ma. You signed the lease, investing in a great deal of time and money. You should be able to live here and enjoy yourself," Sammy concluded.

"And the hell with Rich Flynn," my daughter chimed in.

"Yeah, the hell with the guy," Sammy agreed.

"Okay, then, I'm going to live here and enjoy myself for as long as I can," I said.

"That's the mother we know and love," Sammy said and hugged me.

I took my kids to see the rest of the facility. Afterward, Renée turned to me and said, "I'm more impressed with the place each time I come. It will be a great place for you, Mom. I just know you'll be happy here."

I didn't say what I was thinking. It will be wonderful... if I don't see Rich. Instead, I gave her a wide smile. "What's nice is that I could eat lunch and dinner in the dining room and never cook if I feel like it."

"I wish I could do that," Renée said, and we all laughed.

"The grounds are kept really nice," Sammy said. "Just think you never need someone to mow the lawn or shovel the snow."

"I'm going to hurt my neighbor's son's business."

We all laughed once more.

"What time is your flight, again, Sammy?" I asked.

"9:40. I should be at the airport by 7:40."

"To avoid traffic, we should head towards the airport now and have dinner at a restaurant nearby," Renée suggested.

It's always a pleasure to have my children together. Now it's not as often as I'd like it. I hardly get to see Sammy's kids and look forward to the times that I do. Now that I don't have a house to upkeep, perhaps I can travel more to Maine.

We drove toward the airport and ate at a lovely little restaurant a block away. Following dinner, we said our goodbyes to Sammy at the airport. I tried not to cry but did just the same. I never did like saying goodbye to either child. Despite that, I knew I had to respect them living their own lives with families of their own. It was just easier when Ron was alive.

***

I officially moved in when my bed arrived. After picking up the little things that I'd forgotten to bring at a local department store, it was nearly dinner time. I brought all the packages inside and emptied them. Then I headed out to the dining room. It was already buzzing with activity. I saw that many of the tables were filling up and walked over to one that still had a vacant seat.

"May I sit here?" I asked a group of women. I figured that they might be single like me.

"Of course, you may," said a stately looking brunette who looked to be in her sixties. "My name is Sharon Stahl." Then she went around the table identifying the other four women. Two women could pass for sisters. Both had short silver hair and were thin. The taller of the two was named Mary and the other Carrie. The last woman sitting at the table was slightly overweight with bright red hair. Her name was Louise.

"I'm Marlene Greene and I hope you don't quiz me on your names. Faces I don't forget, but names seem to escape me lately."

"You're not alone," Sharon said. "Have you just moved in here?"

"Yes. In fact, today is my official day."

"That's nice," Louise said. "What's your apartment number?"

"308 B. Are we neighbors?"

"No, but I think you're not too far from Carrie," Louise added.

"You're right above me," Carrie said in a sweet voice.

"Have you had dinner here, yet?" Louise asked.

I shook my head.

"Every table has a waiter or waitress. The menu is displayed in the middle of the table. You select a salad or soup, the main dish from the two or three listed, what you'd like to drink and dessert. Easy, no?" Louise said.

"Can't complain. It's got to beat cooking and doing dishes," I said.

"That's for certain," Carrie's look-alike, Mary, said. It was the first thing she uttered since I sat down.

They sounded like a nice bunch of women and I found myself wanting to get to know them better. I was aware that the assisted living apartments part of the complex had been opened only a year before. The hospital had been already established and the rest of the place was built alongside it. Therefore, these women had only been here during that time period.

The girls had given me a warm welcome and the easy banter continued over coffee and dessert. The laughter was contagious until I felt a hand on my shoulder. I froze, but the other women greeted the man who stood behind me. Yes, it was Rich Flynn. I grit my teeth but said nothing. Instead, Rich said, "I see you're settling in nicely, Marlene and meeting people."

I gave him a forced, but definitely phony smile. Luck was with me, for he didn't ask to join us. "Well have a nice evening, ladies," was all he said and left. I began to breathe easily once more.

Carrie said, "I see you've already met our resident Adonis, Rich Flynn. Isn't he a sexy sweetheart?"

I nearly spit out my coffee. When I recovered my voice I replied, "We went to high school together." Then I stood. "It's been a long day for me and I'm bushed. Thank you all for making my first meal here so pleasant. It was a pleasure meeting you all. Goodnight."

They murmured pleasantries, as well and also bid me goodnight. I left praying that I wasn't accosted by Rich as I made my way to my apartment. Now it had been confirmed. He was a resident here. And as I closed my door behind me, I wondered how I would live here constantly looking over my shoulder.

The following day, when I returned from lunch, I discovered a beautiful flower arrangement left at my apartment door. Then I realized who might have left them there and the beauty of the flowers nearly wilted for me. I couldn't leave the arrangement out there, so I gingerly picked it up and brought it inside. I placed it on the counter and stepped away from it, fearing to read the card attached.

Realizing how silly I was acting, I ripped off the small white envelop and read the card. I shook my head and began to laugh. The flowers had been sent by my kids. I'd been making a mountain out of a molehill, as trite as it sounded. Obviously, Rich didn't care about me one iota— still. He had no remorse, but I was fueling the fire, keeping the entire thing alive. I should finally let the entire fiasco go, once and for all. The only memories I should retain are the ones with Ron and the wonderful life we'd shared.

That night, I was spared the sight of Rich. He wasn't in the dining room and I had dinner with the same women from the previous evening. We all were widows and apparently had a great deal in common. After dinner, we went to the rec hall and played bingo. Following bingo, I returned to my apartment and spoke to my daughter, who'd left a message for me to call her back for a progress report. I thanked her once again for the flowers. After our phone call, I watched some TV and then turned in for the night.

I dreamed I was still in high school. Rich and I had doubled with Bobbie and Joe, our closest friends, on a date. It was summer, so we headed for the beach. After a full day of fun in the sun and surf, we went home and showered and changed, before meeting up for a pizza dinner at our local pizzeria. Afterward, we piled back into our cars and headed for the place the kids called make-out point. It was a secluded area where we could be alone. It was a beautiful night filled with a billion twinkling stars and a glorious full moon, but it could have been pouring cats and dogs and I wouldn't have cared an iota if I was with Rich.

In the backseat, facing one another, Rich looked deeply into my eyes and whispered, "I love you, Marlene, and always will."

"Not as much as I love you," I said, and he leaned over and kissed me.

That kiss morphed into another and each got hotter and steamier until the windows had fogged up completely. All I could see was Rich and the wonderful future that lie ahead of us. Then out of nowhere, a blonde-haired girl about my age rapped on the window.

I woke with a start still remembering the remnants of the dream. I knew all too well who that blonde turned out to be. I swung my legs out of bed and onto the floor. There would be no further sleep for me following that dream. As I padded to the bathroom, it occurred to me that each time I saw Rich he was alone. The woman he married hadn't been with him. I wondered if they divorced or she died. Then again, why should I even care?

I made some breakfast and started my day in an attempt to put all thoughts of Rich and the dream behind me. I went out for a walk around the complex and did some shopping afterward. I met several other residents and was truly settling in. Everyone I met seemed to be around my age and was quite nice.

Miraculously, I didn't see Rich for the next several days. It made it easier to get over my craziness with him. He no longer could take up residence in my head. I was no victim or shrinking violet. It was time to permanently move on, but I hoped I didn't have to test all this new defiance by running into him.

Looking in the mirror as I combed my hair, I realized it was time to get a haircut. There was a hair salon on the premises, so I made an appointment for that same afternoon. The woman sitting in the chair next to me was having her hair dyed. I overheard her ask her hairdresser if she'd heard anything more about the resident who'd been hit by a car as he walked across Main Street. "With the crazy drivers out there, apparently no one is safe."

My ears perked up when I heard that. I truly hoped the person involved was all right. They kept talking, but the name of the victim wasn't revealed. When the dye had been evenly combed through her hair, the woman got up to wait for the dye to take effect. As she passed me, I stopped her.

"Excuse me, I couldn't help but overhear what you were saying about a hit and run. Can you tell me who was hurt?"

"Oh, it's Rich Flynn. So sad, he's such a nice guy."

My throat nearly closed, and my heart rate soared, but I asked the next question. "Is he all right?"

"He's at County general. That's all I know. Sorry."

"Thanks," I replied, sick to my stomach.

I know what you must be thinking. After coming to the conclusion that I had to live my life without a thought about Rich, here I am, worried sick over his condition. Can't I chalk it up to being human? It doesn't erase my feelings about what he'd done to me by any means. It's one thing to be furious with someone for hurting you and another to want to see them get hurt. That's pure evil, which I am not.

I finished having my hair cut and blown dry at the hairdresser under a cloud of worry. Afterward, I drove directly to the hospital. A mental battle had gone on about whether or not I should do this. Somewhere in my head, I had the notion that going to see Rich would somehow give me the closure that apparently, I desperately needed. After all, I never had the chance to tell him how I felt and allow the wound to heal. All this time I merely covered it with a bandage.

As a goodwill measure, I stopped into the gift shop and picked up several male-oriented magazines before going to the main information desk and asking about Rich Flynn. I was directed to the third floor, room 306.

I crowded into an elevator with several other people, including a woman with a walker. As I approached the room Rich was in, I noticed that the door was open. It was dark and quiet inside except for the hissing and beeping of the machines he'd been attached to. I nearly left, but I was so wound up with so many conflicting emotions, that I walked inside.

Rich looked like he was sleeping. If the machines hadn't been working, I would have thought he was dead. His face was a myriad of colors from all the bruising and he had casts on both legs which were raised slightly. His left arm was in a sling, as well. He actually looked like he'd gotten run over by a car.

He must have heard me enter because his eyes snapped open. A half-smile appeared on the part of his face that was flexible. Seeing him like that filled my eyes with tears. I wanted to turn and run away. I would have if he hadn't said, "Marlene? You're the last person I expected to see." His voice was raw and not higher than a whisper.

"I know."

"I'm glad you came, though."

"Really?" I asked.

"There's a great deal that needs to be said. I know how how much I'd hurt you back then and I never truly had a chance to explain."

"Explain?" I said bitterly. "What was there to explain? One day you're telling me how much you love me and always will and the next you're saying goodbye. What could you possibly have to tell me?"

"I could start by telling you how sorry I am?" Rich said.

"Unfortunately, we're well beyond apologies that are just a tad too late," I said, but there was something in his eyes that made me let him finish, so I stopped haranguing him.

"Can you pour me a little water, please. My throat is so dry."

I reached over and poured some of the water from his pitcher into the cup with the bendable straw. Rich reached over and held it with his good hand. I stood there to help him if he needed it. He took several long pulls on the straw and put the cup back down.

"My Dad was a businessman through and through. Sometimes my mom wondered if he loved his business more than the family. I fear she was right. It turned out back then that he wanted to merge or acquire a rival business. He made overtures to the CEO but was rebuffed. That only made my dad try harder.

"That's when he came up with his brilliant plan that destroyed both of us."

"What are you getting at, Rich?"

"It turns out that the other CEO had a daughter around our age. My old man got it into his head that if I married the daughter, then the businesses could be united by marriage. The only problem was that I didn't want to marry this girl. I loved you. It didn't matter to me if she was pretty and extremely rich. I only had eyes for you.

"Only my father didn't care. Love didn't matter. I'd grow to love her. We fought and finally, he threatened to cut me off financially. I still didn't agree."

So, what made you change your mind?" I asked.

"He threatened to kick my mother to the curb, as well. That I couldn't let him do. She had just been diagnosed with leukemia."

"I had no idea," I said. "I'm sorry to hear that."

"Ironically, the marriage was a disaster and I grew to loathe my wife. She was a spoiled rich girl, selfish in every way. The two years I remained with her was like living in hell. The only comfort I ever got was the fact that you found someone else and married him. I take it you had a happy marriage?"

"How did you know?"

"I never stopped loving you and hired an investigator to find you, Marlene."

The tears slipped from my eyes. "Yes. Ron was a good man and a great father to our kids. I loved him, but it wasn't the same kind of love that I had had with you. Did you ever remarry?"

Rich shook his head. "I only wanted you and no one else could compare."

I whisked away my tears. "I don't know what to say. All these years I honestly hated you for breaking up with me. Now I feel all that was wasted emotion."

"Hey, we're human, right?"

I sighed.

"Listen, Marlene, when I get out of here, why don't you cut me some slack and allow me to make it up to you," Rich suggested. "Afterall, everyone in our complex thinks I'm a nice guy."

I laughed and nodded.

"You know, it's been said that there is a thin line between love and hate," Rich added.

"That's so true. It explains my reaction all these years."

"No matter what, we can at least be friends."

"I definitely think so," I said, placing my hand on his.

"And maybe— just maybe, a little more," he said and winked.

When he did that, I saw the young guy I once loved with all my heart and wondered if we could turn back the hands of time together.

THE END

**Other Titles by Candace Gold**
The Twist of Fate
The Promise
A Heated Romance
Crazy Love

Reverie
And Justice for All
I Confess
The Greatest Gift of All
Raped by the Law
Return to Hell
I was Stalked by my Own Man
Under a Kinder Moon
Twisted Love
Summer Rain
Left to Die

### About the Author

With nearly 200 short stories, numerous anthologies, novellas and novels in print, whether she's writing less edgy contemporary romance, or spicy hot erotica as Candy Caine, she keeps her husband, Robert, on his toes in their Arizona home. Supportive with her writing career, he's always willing to help her add authenticity to the scenes in her stories. After all, technique is so important for good writing. Her biggest thrill is to bring the joy of reading to others.